MW01687173

The Average of Deviance

K. Simpson

Fortitude Press, Inc.
Austin • Texas

Published by Fortitude Press, Inc., Austin, Texas. For further information about this or other titles, please contact Fortitude Press, Inc., P.O. Box 41, Melbourne, FL 32902, or visit our website at www.fortitudepress.com.

ISBN: 0-9718150-1-1

First Edition, March 2002
Printed in the United States of America

Edited by Anne Brisk
Technical edits by Medora MacDougall
Book and cover design by Ryan Daly
Web design by Mya Smith

The Average of Deviance

Acknowledgements

You wouldn't be reading this book at all if Shaun Day, Maureen Sak and Ian Rowan hadn't read it first. Thanks also to Nancy Amazon & Ewok, Anne Brisk, Medora MacDougall, Ryan Daly and the Devil's Workshop list, who think it would actually be a *good* thing if I wrote faster.

For Vic Nelson, who expected me to write a book someday.
Bet he never expected this one.

Preface

My name is Devlin Kerry, and I have a demon. You probably do, too, but mine is on the outside. And no amount of therapy is going to make her go away.

It all started a few months ago. Technically, you could say it started any number of times — when I went into advertising in the first place, say, or when I met Cassie — but the actual demon part is new. I was just minding my own business one day, and the next thing I knew, *she* was there. She's never quite gone away. Cassie hates that.

"It's your own fault," she always says. "I *told* you celibacy was unnatural. You can't go around *not* sleeping with people and not expect to get into trouble."

Turned out that the people Cassie was mad at me for not sleeping with was her. I didn't know that then, though. As far as I *did* know, you couldn't sleep with your best friend even if you wanted to, especially if you were both girls, particularly if you were both straight.

That's where Monica came in. She's a demon. She's also kind of ...

Well, sexy. Very, as a matter of fact. I really couldn't help it.

Cassie hates that, too.

∞ ∞ ∞

It's all kind of hard to explain, but I'll try. You might as well have the whole backstory before you go any further.

I'm in advertising, like I said — associate creative director at J/J/G Advertising. It's all over town that the place is a madhouse, which is true and mostly the fault of the man who runs it. Jenner is crazier than the rest of us put together.

But as crazy as we are at J/J/G, we're also good, if I do say so myself. For an agency in a middle-market city in the Midwest, we do all right. On the rare days when I'm still proud of what I do, I'm proud to work there.

Even though my unofficial title is associate creative director in charge of sex.

That's not my fault. I just happened to write a few commercials with a little spin on them, and then I came down with this *rep*. I was celibate at the time, though, and had been for six years. Everyone says I wrote those ads *because* I was celibate — repressing my sex drive, sublimating, that sort of thing. Everyone says it also accounted for my temper.

I have an undeserved rep for that, too. Just because I whacked a slow coffeemaker with a stapler once — just once! — doesn't mean I'm a monster.

But never mind all that. The important thing is the celibacy thing, because it caused the demon. You know what they say: You get what you ask for, even if you don't know you've asked.

Yes, I slept with her. Eventually. I wouldn't have known that it was even possible, because I'd never slept with anything in a female shape before, let alone a demon. Let's just say Monica gave me an education.

And then she did something really diabolical: She put Cassie and me together. Turns out that Cassie'd been repressing something, too. My beautiful, blonde best friend, the superyuppie femme fatale, the woman who could (and did) get any man she ever wanted — against all odds, she wanted me instead.

So Monica made a deal with her. (At the agency's Halloween party, which was Monica's idea of irony.) The deal was that Cassie wouldn't let me get all repressed again, and Monica would go away. Cassie didn't know yet what a demon's word is worth, so she agreed. But at least Monica took off for a while.

A very short while. And that led to what follows.

Consider it a warning about mixing sex, advertising and demons. One is bad, two is worse and three is the state of my life.

Chapter One

November 1
Early Friday Morning

Somewhere, a phone was ringing. The best thing to do about ringing phones was nothing, so I did. Besides, I was too comfortable to move at the moment, dug into a nice warm bed with a naked blonde wrapped around me, just like the dream I'd been having. It had been an insane sort of dream, really — something about a Halloween party, a six-foot condom, a contagious fistfight and a sexy demon, none of which made any sense. But it had ended in a wild night with an angel who was still asleep all over me, and I was starting to think I liked it.

Blessed silence fell as voice mail picked up. I pulled the angel closer in my dream and started to drift back off. Now, where were we?

The phone started ringing again.

"If you love me," the angel murmured, "you'll make that stop."

With one hand, still asleep, I felt for the phone on the night table, picked up the receiver and slammed it back down. Twenty seconds or so of peace. Then the phone rang again. The angel said a very bad word, and my eyes shot open.

It wasn't a dream. There really *was* a naked blonde in my bed, and unless I was completely crazy...

She pushed up off me, glanced at the phone and gave me her most ominous look. "You could get celibate again in a hurry," she said.

No, I wasn't crazy. It was Cassie, all right. Did that mean that last night had really happened? *All* of it? My bewilderment must have shown, because she finally just shook her head and reached over me to grab the phone. "Kerry residence. *What?!?*"

Whoever was on the other end started laughing, and she dropped the receiver as though it were hot. "It's for you. And I do mean 'it.' "

That could only mean my least-favorite copywriter and practically least-favorite person. I made another mental note to fire him soon. "Kurt, damn you, what do you want?"

"You mean besides a videotape of last night?" He laughed even harder. "You *did* make one, didn't you? It would make a great recruiting film for lesbianism. Even better than *Basic Instinct*. Can't say much for you, boss, but Cassie's about as hot as that Sharon Stone babe."

Apparently, Cassie heard that, because she muttered, "Hotter."

"Kurt," I said dangerously, "you've got ten seconds."

"All right, all right. I just called to warn you that Jack's on his way over, and you snap at me like —"

Instinctively, I pushed Cassie away. She gave me a very bad look and snuggled back up. "He'd better not be," I said to Kurt. "We called in sick today."

"Well, boss, there's a school of thought about that. About half the agency would agree with you on the 'sick' part. Of course, *I* don't think it's sick. I think it's a very beautiful thing. What are you both wearing right now?"

Exasperated, Cassie took the receiver away and reached over me again to tap the speakerphone button. "Devvy doesn't think very fast first thing in the morning. She *should* have told you to stop playing adolescent games with us and go play with yourself instead. I'll just bet you need the practice. Now, if that's all you wanted ..."

"Cassie," he said, "I'm hurt. I'm only trying to help. I thought you might both want to put some clothes on before Jack gets there — that's all. If *I* don't get to see it, why should he?"

Well, she'd tried reason. "All right," I said. "We'll pretend to believe you. *Why* is Jack coming over?"

"Kester Mortuaries. We've got to show the tape at 11:00. Jenner wants you both there."

I glanced over at the alarm clock. 9:09. "You and Heather did the creative. Cassie gave Chip the account-exec part. Why would *we* need to be there?"

"Well, you don't, really," Kurt admitted. "But it came straight from Jenner. He's sending Jack over to make sure you both show up." His grin was almost audible over the phone line. "God, you should've seen Jack's face. Getting sent out on errands like a water boy. *My* guess is that it's payback for that rumble last night."

"That would be about Jenner's speed." Interested in spite of myself, I lowered my voice in the vain hope that Cassie wouldn't hear. "So who won the fight? Did anybody lose any body parts?"

I really *did* hate myself for asking. It wasn't every Halloween that the head of an advertising agency dressed up like a glow-in-the-dark condom and got into a fistfight with his creative director, but weirder things had happened at J/J/G. In fact, I'd been involved in most of them. It was a good thing Jenner could never remember my name.

"Well, Jenner *was* a body part last night," Kurt said, "and the general opinion is that he lost on points, but —"

"It was probably because of all that latex. I hear that's why men hate condoms — they cut off the flow of blood to their brains."

Cassie smacked me on the head. "Stop that. I don't sleep with trolls."

It was pure habit, but my answer was, "Since when?"

"Starting as soon as I get out of this bed," she snapped.

Kurt started laughing again. "A match made in heaven. Or somewhere. You'd better start getting decent, by the way. Jack left here fifteen minutes ago."

Cassie and I exchanged glances while we did the math. My condo was fifteen minutes from J/J/G, which meant ...

Well, for starters, it meant she had about thirty seconds to find her angel costume, which was probably down in the living room somewhere. She promptly leaped out of bed and made for the stairs.

"You could have told us that sooner," I complained to Kurt, fishing my robe out of the sheets.

"Sure, I could have. But I promised Jack I'd wait to call you till he was almost there."

I was still processing that treachery when the doorbell rang.

"I heard that," he said. "Too bad you won't have time now to cover up those bite marks. Cassie *does* bite, doesn't she? Have a nice day."

I grabbed the receiver, slammed it down as hard as humanly possible and then raced down the stairs. But it was too late; Cassie had the door open already.

"Where's Kerry?" Jack demanded.

"Right behind her," I said — and stopped short as I caught sight of what was on the doorstep. Jack was not a thing of beauty on his best days, and this was nowhere near one of them. Even though he was wearing a nice suit, and even though he was about as well-groomed as a man with hair plugs could be, he looked as though he'd been run through a Cuisinart. For the second time that morning, I regretted having missed that fight.

"We'll talk about how I look later," he said to me. "I figure it's your fault, so I *promise* you we'll talk. But first, there's that Kester meeting at 11:00. Jenner's calling you both in."

"We called in sick," I said. "As in not going to work, no matter how many creative directors he sends over here to play fetch. So —"

"Forget it, Kerry. You don't have a choice." He gave me a most unpleasant smile, or what might have been a smile; it was hard to tell for sure with his lip split like that. "If you don't show, I get to fire you, and Kurt gets your job."

I started laughing. "My job? You bet. He can have it, you stupid, hair-challenged son of —"

Cassie instantly put both hands over my mouth. "We'll be there. Thank you. You can go now."

He finished scowling at me and then turned on her. "Be a few minutes early, and don't even *think* about touching each other in front of the client."

Annoyed, I shook Cassie off, a few choice words on the tip of my tongue, but Jack was already halfway back to his Jag in the driveway. He appeared to be limping on both sides. Distracted, I watched him struggle to open and then close the driver's-side door.

"I wonder what Jenner looks like this morning, if Jack looks like that," I mused.

"We'll find out soon enough. Come here. We've still got time."

"For what?"

For answer, she kissed me with obvious intent.

Distantly, I heard metal crunch on metal out in the driveway. A check confirmed it: Jack had just plowed his Jag into my mailbox. Cassie probably should have thought to close the door first.

"I left it open on purpose," she said. "I knew he'd look. Serves the stupid, hair-challenged son of a bitch right. Now, where were we?"

∞ ∞ ∞

Going to the office on this particular morning after was ... interesting. I wasn't big on interesting under the circumstances. No sooner did Cassie and I hit the lobby than people started making a big point of Not Looking. Oh, they checked us out, all right, but they didn't want to get caught at it, so they were all Not Looking as hard as they could.

You'd think they'd never seen us before. We were dressed the way we always dressed for work. We didn't have horns, hooves or tails. We didn't even show any visible signs of the night before, which I suppose was what they were all looking for. But the scrutiny was still annoying.

Walt and a few copywriters were just getting off the elevator when we were getting on. The copywriters did their best to act normal, but Walt had never committed a normal act in his life and wasn't about to start. He grabbed us both and tried to bear-hug us at the same time.

"I love you two," he said fervently. "I won five hundred bills on you last night. So was it as good for both of you as it was for me?"

Cassie thwacked him in a certain place with her attaché and pulled me into the elevator.

"Keep me posted!" he called as the doors started to close. "I've got another $200 on when the baby's due!"

Things were going to get interesting, all right, starting right about now.

∞ ∞ ∞

We made sure to walk into the conference room at exactly one minute till 11:00. Everyone else was already seated, and as we entered, they stared at us like so many owls.

"Good morning, everyone," Cassie said sweetly, with her most innocent expression — and then jabbed me in the ribs. *Right. Smile.* With a little effort, I did.

Then I got a good look at Jenner and a second look at Jack, and the smile turned into the real thing. Cassie saw that and shot me a warning glance as we took our chairs — the only two left and very far apart.

"Mr. Kester," Jack said to the client, who was seated directly across from me, "I don't know whether you've met our caboose here. The lovely blonde is Cassandra Wolfe. She's your account manager, you lucky son of a gun. And the evil-looking dark one —"

"Devlin Kerry, Mr. Kester," I interrupted, reaching across the table.

The client grudgingly shook my hand. He had a grip like a sick flounder, only wetter. It went with his face, though. Idly, I pictured the man in a fish tank, with those few strands of black hair and the tiny mustache slicked down too tightly to move in the current. I wondered what his parents had looked like and why they hadn't thrown each other back. I wondered ...

"I remember you," the client said. "You spat coffee at me a couple of months ago."

There was an epidemic of coughing and throat-clearing around the conference table. Quickly, I ran through my options. The most amusing one was to stare at him blankly, so I did.

"You got off light, Mr. Kester," Jack said solemnly. "She usually gouges clients' eyes out. That's only if she *likes* them. See what she did to Mr. Jenner and me last night? If she'd been in a *bad* mood at the time, she'd have —"

"That's enough, Harper," Jenner said to him.

"But, sir —"

"Business before pleasure, Harper."

Jack sighed. "Yes, sir."

The client gave me another nervous look. I continued to stare at him.

"We'll see the tape now," Jenner said. "Derry, stop staring at the client."

"Eventually, sir," I replied.

Next to me, Heather didn't quite manage to cover her giggling fit, and the client turned all the way sideways in his chair to avoid my eye. Satisfied, I shifted attention to the TV monitor, where the Kester

Mortuaries commercial was starting to run.

It was a bad one, even for one that Kurt and Heather hadn't wanted to do. True, my team should never have had the account — Walt's group usually got this sort of thing — but Jack had lost a fight with his wife the night before and was feeling vengeful, so he gave it to us. Kurt had happened to annoy me that day, so I'd given him the job personally. After he wrote three drafts of a parody of the "Thriller" video, which was his idea of spite, I finally put Heather on the account, too. She hadn't spoken to me for two days.

That cycle of violence explained, pretty much, what we were seeing on the screen: soft-focus vignettes of Family Life with a scrawny little undertaker smack in the middle of all of them. Kester at a wedding. Kester at a child's birthday party. Kester at Thanksgiving dinner, God help me, carving the turkey. There was no narration, but no one could have heard narration anyway, what with all those violins on the soundtrack. Finally, amid a great wash of strings, we hit the title frames — "Kester Mortuaries: A Friend of the Family" — and the agony was over.

Careful to keep our expressions neutral, we all turned to the client, who was chewing his lip thoughtfully. "It still isn't quite my vision," he finally said.

Not quite his vision. Not quite the mortician's vision. I felt a silly grin start to grow on my face.

"Trade me places," Cassie said abruptly to Heather.

Heather took one look and traded without comment. As Cassie settled in, she slipped her hand under the table, placed it way up my thigh — and dug her fingernails in hard. Which sobered me right up.

"Whatever you just did, Miss Wolfe," Jenner said, "you're in charge of her for the rest of the meeting."

"My pleasure," Cassie said. "Now, you were saying, Mr. Kester ...?"

The client started his litany of complaint, and I forcibly removed Cassie's hand. She put it back, without clawing this time. I pushed it off again, harder. We were in a meeting, for God's sake ... and besides, Kurt was watching.

"... took the liberty of bringing a tape along," the client was saying, "to give you an idea of what I'm looking for. Would it be all right if we play it?"

"Please," Jenner said. For a second, I thought he'd winked at the client. Hard to tell, as black as that eye was, but strange just the same.

At first, we saw only a grainy black-and-white scene shot from a strange angle — probably shot on a security camera, judging by the way the footage looked. There were two people in the center of the shot, or maybe just one; if there were two, they were awfully close together. I squinted to get better focus.

Then I got focus, and my heart stopped cold. This footage had come off a security camera, all right, and it had been shot last night at the Halloween party. Specifically, it had been shot right around midnight in a storage room, which was where Cassie and I had kissed for the first time.

All I could do was watch the screen in horror. I'd been there, of course, but damn, I didn't remember the kiss going on that long or being so ...

Well, so *hot*. It was just the kind of thing you wouldn't want to watch with your mother in the room — let alone your colleagues, your bosses and a client — and it was probably not the kind of thing you would ever hear the end of, if you'd been involved. Cassie was going to *kill* me.

For what seemed like forever, there was dead quiet in the room. Finally, Kurt cleared his throat.

"*That* ought to move a few caskets," he drawled.

That was all it took. They broke up completely, howling and pounding the table — even the client. Shocked, I stared at him for real this time.

"We've been had, Devvy," Cassie said softly.

"Looks that way."

"If I asked you nicely, *would* you gouge their eyes out? For me?"

"Of course I would."

"And if I asked you to start with Mr. Kester ...?"

With an evil smile, I scraped my chair back. The client yelped and ducked behind Jenner.

"Well, you *did* spit coffee at me," he protested.

"You wanted sex in a mortuary ad," I explained. "You were lucky I didn't whack you upside that little head. Which eye do you want me to start with, Cass?"

Jenner, imperious, held up a hand. "I think that'll do, people. Thank you, Mr. Kester, for playing along. Thank you, Derry, for the Godzilla impression. And thank *you*, Mr. Wheeler, for the idea. Very creative. I may have to promote you one of these days."

Kurt was the happiest creature alive at that moment. Jack seemed to be feeling good, too; he gave Kurt a big male-bonding backslap and leaned over to say something private. Whatever it was, both of them found it hilarious.

"That's it," Cassie said. "We're leaving. Come on, Devvy."

Jenner looked puzzled. "You're leaving? But this was just payback. We're all square now. You don't mean you're quitting, do you?"

I did and was about to, but Cassie jumped in. "We'll think about it over the weekend. We'll be busy the rest of today, talking to lawyers. I wouldn't sleep much between now and Monday, if I were any of you.

Have a terrible day."

"She can't threaten us, can she, Harper?" Jenner asked.

"She can try," Jack said. "Don't worry about it. My mother-in-law is part-gorilla. She could beat them both up."

"Maybe she's part-dyke instead," Kurt suggested.

Jack shrugged. "What's the difference?"

At the door, I pulled Cassie to a stop and regarded my colleagues one by one in icy silence. Only Jenner, Jack and Kurt were happy now; everyone else, even the client, seemed to be ashamed. I made a mental note to remember that Chip hadn't wanted to play along. One ally was better than none.

"It's too late to be hanged for sheep, Cass," I said, "so we might as well be hanged for wolves. May I?"

She read my mind and smiled. "I was hoping you would."

So I drew her into a long, stagy kiss. She gave as good as she got, and then some. It was as close to the security-camera tape as we could manage, but it was close enough; I don't think a soul in the conference room breathed until we broke it off. Live performance *is* always more involving than TV, after all.

"That wasn't funny, Derry," Jenner complained.

"Kerry," I corrected. "And if you ever pull anything like that tape again, this is going to seem like Monty Fucking Python by comparison."

Cassie instantly pulled me out of the room. She kept hold of my arm as we made our way down the hall. The gesture was more damage control than affection, but it caused everyone we passed to Not Look.

" 'Monty Fucking Python'?" she asked.

"Don't start with me. I didn't get much sleep."

"Neither did I. Do you hear me complaining?"

"I wasn't complaining."

"Good. So I won't start with you. But you're lucky I love you."

"Very lucky," I agreed. "And incidentally, same to you, lady."

We exchanged an intimate smile, which made an intern with an armful of storyboards crash into a wall. Cassie looked at him as though he were an insect. Then she turned back to me. "Just so I'll know, what did you mean by what you said about Monty Python?"

"I have no idea. Want to come along for the ride and find out?"

"Can't wait," she said.

Chapter Two

My car was still parked outside the club where J/J/G had held the party, so Cassie drove me there; then we went our separate ways. One good thing about being involved with a friend, she explained, was that you didn't necessarily have to be nice all the time.

"Give me a day," she said as I walked around the car to say goodbye. "I don't want to get sick and tired of you yet."

"Right back atcha."

"My place tomorrow night?"

"What time?"

"Doesn't matter — it's for all night. Now go away, Devvy, before I have to kill you."

I laughed and tapped her car door in lieu of a goodbye kiss. Then I just stood on the sidewalk and watched the BMW drive off, tires screeching. Cassie was unsafe at every speed — and that was just fine with me now.

∞ ∞ ∞

Something ringing woke me for the second time that day. Pulling both pillows over my head, I went all the way under the covers. The alarm was set for 8:00 Saturday morning, which was still twelve hours away, and not even grizzly bears were getting me out of bed before then.

The ringing was followed by knocking, and the knocking was followed by more ringing. The grizzly bears were going to have to do better than that. Yawning, I burrowed all the way down to the foot of the bed.

Then a hideous sound outside began to rattle the bedroom window. It took about ten seconds to identify it: William Shatner, singing "Mr. Tambourine Man." Flinging the covers in all directions, I shot out of bed and stormed to the window with murder in my heart.

To my surprise, though, the monster on the lawn with the tape player wasn't Kurt or Jack, but Troy. He shut off the machine the instant he saw me and flashed his most winning smile — the one that made him look like Tom Cruise, the one he knew I couldn't resist. It was a cruel god that stuck me with him for an art director. Muttering curses, I opened the window.

"Sorry," he called up. "Heather's idea."

"You'd better be here to apologize for a lot more than that."

"We are. Can we come in?"

I considered. "You. Not the tape."

"Wouldn't be caught dead with it. See you at the front door?"

I slammed the window shut and went down to let him, Heather and Chip in. At least they'd been smart enough to bring a couple of pizzas along. They followed me to the kitchen like ducklings and settled around the table while I opened a bottle of wine.

"About this morning," Chip began.

"I'm listening."

"We're really sorry. It wasn't our idea. We wanted you to know that."

With the ghost of a smile, I handed him the first glass. "I know that. You wouldn't be here if you were guilty."

"We're sorry about last night, too," Heather added.

"Last night's another story. *That*, we'll need to talk about. But Cassie's not here, so it'll have to wait. In the meantime, who do I thank for the pizza?"

They all relaxed visibly. "See, I told you she wouldn't bite," Heather said to the others.

"Bet she does, though," Troy said. "Bet if we asked Cassie —"

Heather smacked him on the arm, and he froze as he heard what he'd just said.

"Way to go, boy," Chip growled.

I leaned back against the counter and took a long draft of wine, rather enjoying their discomfort. It wasn't much, but even a little payback is payback.

Troy threw up his hands in disgust. "Dev, I'm sorry. Kurt gets contagious sometimes, you know?"

"Don't insult me with lame excuses. This has to be the only thing anyone's talked about all day. Why wouldn't you make jokes? Why stop now?"

Heather frowned slightly. "I don't like this. She almost sounds reasonable."

"Cass and I talked about it a little," I continued. "She thinks we can't expect much better. She's not even sure we deserve it, because if it had been anyone else, we'd have been making jokes, too. What goes around, comes around, and it just came around, so we're going to have to live with it for a while."

"I *really* don't like this," Heather said, looking genuinely worried.

"Maybe she's just in a good mood," Troy suggested. "I heard she was in a good mood once, a couple of years before I started at the agency. It could happen again."

He followed that with another of those Tom Cruise smiles, so I gave up and smiled back.

"More relaxed now, are you?" he asked, encouraged. "Less tension today?"

"Troy!" Heather wailed as Chip punched him in the shoulder.

"Much less tension," I said, fighting to keep from laughing. "Thank you for asking. I'd always heard that it worked for that. Somebody ought to bottle it. They'd make a fortune."

"Yeah, and *you'd* handle the campaign," Heather said.

I decided to give them one last tweak. "Why not? I've got firsthand knowledge of the product. You might even say I have ... specialized knowledge."

"You've probably got lipstick in some really specialized places, too," Troy remarked.

Startled by a possibility that I'd never considered, even though I'd showered that morning, I started to check — and then scowled. They were all laughing like well-dressed hyenas. Chip, though, had the decency to look a little guilty about it.

"My bad," I growled. "Walked right into that one, didn't I?"

Heather finally got a grip. "Sorry. Really. I mean it. But God, it's just so hard *not* to do this."

"Never mind me. You'd better not even think about giving Cassie this kind of trouble. You *are* going over to apologize to her, too, aren't you?"

"Of course," Chip said. "I report to her."

"Is one of the pizzas for her?"

"Nope. She gets dessert."

That didn't seem fair. "What kind?"

"Turtle cheesecake. She loves it."

Definitely not fair. "Well, so do I. How about just one little —"

Heather snorted. "She said you'd try. She told me to smack you if you did."

"Won't kill her to share. If it's a whole ... wait. When did she tell you that?"

"I stopped by her place right before I picked the guys up. When I called —"

"You called *her*, but you just dropped in here?"

"Well," Chip said, "it's like this. We figured you'd be in bed, and we figured you wouldn't want to get up, and we knew Cassie had that *Golden Throats* tape ..."

Of course she did. How could I have forgotten? A few years ago, she'd ordered it from a catalog on a whim. I hated when she got whims. The day after the tape came, I was out of the office on a shoot, so she called my voice mail over and over to leave little samples. The Shatner had been bad, but the Leonard Nimoy had been unbelievable. Especially "Proud Mary." Tina Turner should've beamed him somewhere for that one.

"We *are* sorry about the tape," Troy said to me.

"No, you're not. But Cass is in trouble with me now for letting you have it."

Chip looked surprised. "You mean you two are still going to fight?"

"Of course we're still going to fight. We're still friends."

"That sounds so wrong somehow," Heather mused. "But for the two of you, it's perfect. Just like the two of you finally getting together is perfect."

Some wine went down the wrong way; Troy leaped up to whack me on the back, which I ignored. "What do you mean 'perfect'?"

"Oh, cut it out," she said. "You and Cassie are made for each other. We all knew it ages ago. Why do you think we're having so much fun with this?"

"You knew it ages ago?" I repeated.

They exchanged tolerant little smirks. "It isn't rocket science," she explained. "There was always all this *tension* between you two, and you were always, always fighting with each other. What else could it be but love? You *do* love each other, Dev."

I shifted uncomfortably against the counter. She was right, and Cassie and I had already said the L word to each other, but I wasn't sure how I felt about having it out in public like this.

"My God," Troy said. "I believe you hit a nerve, Dr. McIntyre. The patient is fidgeting."

"I'm not fidgeting. I'm hungry. Are these pizzas for decoration or what?"

Chip obediently opened a box and handed me a slice. But he ruined the nice gesture by winking.

"Maybe it's the word," Troy continued. "The associate creative director in charge of sex might not have a clue about love."

"Don't go there," I warned. "Dammit, Troy, I used to like you."

"You still do. And *I* like *you*, so I'm going to do you a favor. When are you seeing her again?"

"Tomorrow night. But what does that —"

"Good. Got just the thing." He reached for his wallet and dug out a business card. "Here you go. Ask for Jane, and tell her I sent you."

I turned the card over, expecting to find writing on the back, but it was blank. "I think you gave me the wrong card. This is from a florist shop."

"Sure is. Tell Jane you want a dozen long-stemmed white roses, no thorns, and my discount. White, Dev — not red. Everybody does red. White's more original. Besides, it stands for —"

"I am *not* sending her flowers," I said to him.

Chip cleared his throat. "Well, no, you don't want to *send* them. You want to give them to her in person."

"Send, give — same difference. I'm not —"

"Trust me," Chip said earnestly.

I regarded him in silence.

"It's the first time after the first time," Heather said. "It's important."

"But this is *Cassie* we're talking about, dammit. If I lose my mind and take her flowers, she'll —"

"She'll ask who you are and what you've done with Dev," Heather said. "I know. She might even laugh, considering that it's you. But *then* she'll thank you, and I guarantee you'll like how."

Troy leaned over, interested. "Really?"

She shoved him back out of her space. "A dozen white roses. Got that?"

Well, I had the card, anyway. For safekeeping, I put it in my pajama pocket. "I hope you don't give Cassie any crazy advice."

"She doesn't need it," she said. "Now, how about giving us some forks before the pizza gets cold?"

∞ ∞ ∞

After they left, I went back to bed, but sleep was out of the question. So I just lay there watching the ceiling fan and wondering what I'd gotten myself into now.

It had all happened so fast last night. There'd barely been time to react, let alone think. One minute, Cassie and I had been friends; one minute later, we'd been a lot more, and what did that make us now? Were we dating? Were we experimenting? Was I really going to have to buy her roses?

The flowers themselves weren't the issue. If Cassie wanted roses — hell's fire, if she wanted a greenhouse's worth of them — I'd get them for her. The problem was that it was going to feel very *guy*. Did there really have to be a guy in this relationship? And if so, why would it have to be me? As girlie as Cass was, she could probably clean my clock any time she pleased. I didn't much like knowing that.

Scowling at the fan blades, I remembered something that Walt and Kurt had said about the only known gay person at J/J/G.

"Connie the Barbarian's not really a girl," Walt had insisted. "Not even if you turn her over and look, like you do on a dog. So I don't see how she can be a lezzie."

Kurt had laughed. "Banging girls is a pretty good clue."

"But that's just it, Wheeler — the Barbarian's a *guy*. How can she be a dyke if she's a guy?"

"Well, what if whatever she's banging looks just like her? Wouldn't that be two dykes?"

"Exactly," Walt had said triumphantly. "Dykes *are* guys. So you've either got a girl and a guy, or you've got two guys. You see a lezzie in any of that?"

Kurt had whistled in wonder. "Teach me, master."

All right, they were low lifes. But so was I, because I'd laughed. Which made me every bit as bad as ...

The phone rang.

"Damn," I said but grabbed it. "Hello?"

There was brief silence at the other end; then music started playing. Not just any music, but "Like a Virgin."

I checked Caller ID and collapsed in helpless, stupid laughter. Cassie was crazier than I was.

And just for that, the woman was going to get a few flowers.

Chapter Three

Saturday

Saturday was a good day, in that nothing interesting happened. With no demons, friends or brand-new loves around, I got to sleep late and then catch up on chores, which may not sound like much unless you've been overscheduled for weeks. (I had been and was seriously starting to think about getting an unlisted life.) I even had time to surf the Web for fun for the first time in a while. There was a sweater on the J. Crew site that I'd had my eye on, for one thing. True, we had a J. Crew store at the mall, but where was the challenge in that?

I took the PowerBook downstairs, put a Cowboy Junkies disc in the CD player and turned on the TV to catch up on elective multitasking. With one eye on "Bugs Bunny and Company," I checked e-mail. The inbox was jammed, but only one mail was worth reading.

> Devvy,
>
> You are in such trouble. I woke up today with a sappy love song in my head, and I *never* get like this. I think something's wrong with me.
>
> Something had better be wrong with you, too, if you get my drift.
>
> Can you be here at 7:00?
>
> C
>
> P.S.: I love you.

On the TV screen, Wile E. Coyote got whacked with an anvil. I knew the feeling.

> Cass —
>
> Be there at 6:59.
>
> — D
>
> P.S. — Love you back.

"Ruining my own rep," I muttered, but sent it anyway.

Then I switched off the Mac, the CD player and the TV, and went for a walk in the rain. Didn't bother with an umbrella. I felt like getting wet.

∞ ∞ ∞

Having promised, I pulled into Cassie's drive at 6:59 sharp. The house was dark except for faint light in the downstairs windows, and the porch light was off, but I knew the way. Parcel in hand, I took the curved flagstone path to the door and rang the bell.

She opened the door right away. I couldn't really see her, silhouetted the way she was against the dim light inside, but she smelled sensational.

Then it hit me: I was nervous.

"Avon calling," I said experimentally.

"Oh, damn. I was expecting Devvy. Have you seen her? Kind of tall, kind of dark, kind of good-looking, in a Deadhead-with-credit-cards way ..."

We both just stood there for a second. Now I was really, *really* nervous ... and by her voice, so was she.

"Can I come in? It's raining."

Her answer was a kiss — one of those long ones, with a lot of spin. Eventually, I helped. We shouldn't have done that on the front steps, probably, but it certainly broke the ice.

"Wow," I finally said.

"Wow yourself. Now get in here. It's raining."

I followed her into the living room, which was lit only by a fire, and drew a sharp breath when she turned. She was wearing a silk jumpsuit in a blue that came close to the color of her eyes, unbuttoned rather far down, and a thin gold chain disappeared down the front of it just where things got interesting. Things were interesting everywhere, to be honest; the jumpsuit really followed her form. It all worked. She was knockout gorgeous.

And she'd chosen me. That wasn't possible.

Was it?

Whatever was on my face at that moment, it made her smile. Not in any of the ways I was used to, but a slow, sexy smile that made my pulse race. No one had ever looked at me like that before, not even Monica — not that she counted.

"You don't need the raincoat now," she said.

Or anything else you're wearing, her tone added.

I swallowed hard and brought the parcel out from behind my back.

"If you'll take this, I'll hang it up."

"What's in it?"

"Open it and see."

She took it, and I went to the hall closet. Briefly, I considered hanging up my blazer, too. I'd put on the same thing I'd worn to work Friday, out of superstition, and felt overdressed.

But then again, Heather might have been right; maybe the first time after the first time *was* important. Besides, Cassie had on Date Earrings and Date Shoes, so maybe I was underdressed instead.

I started to shut the door — and got all but tackled into the closet by Cassie, who wrapped herself around me and held on.

"Does this mean you like the flowers?"

"I like the flowers," she said, as her hands began to travel.

"Cass?"

"Mmm?"

"We're in a closet."

"Mm-hmm."

"You don't think that's a little ironic?"

"It's a big closet," she said. "We don't ever have to come out."

∞ ∞ ∞

We weren't animals, of course; we were civilized, adult human beings who knew they had all night. Besides, the doorbell rang right then, which ruined the mood. It was the delivery man from Szechwan Garden with dinner.

So Cassie put the roses in a vase, and we had dinner out of cartons in the firelight with a bottle of Riesling. The whole thing was familiar and oddly comforting; we'd had many dinners together over the years, some of them in this very living room. This, I could handle. My nerves slowly began to settle down, and she seemed to be more relaxed herself.

But every so often, she would smile just a little too long, or I would not-quite-accidentally touch her, and sparks flew. We were definitely not in Kansas anymore.

When we finished, Cassie handed me one of the fortune cookies. "You know what they say about fortune cookies. Whatever your fortune is, you have to add 'in bed' at the end."

"You're making that up."

"I am not. See for yourself."

I shrugged and cracked the cookie open. The paper strip inside said, "You will travel to distant lands." Without a word, I handed it to her.

She laughed. "Not like that puts any pressure on me. But maybe I'm getting off easy. Read mine."

I took the fortune, which read, "Your heart's desire is at hand."

"You're right. No pressure at all." I held out one hand for her crumbled cookie and dropped it into an empty carton along with the remains of mine; neither of us ever ate the things. "So what *is* your heart's desire?"

"In bed?"

"Anywhere."

"Devvy, honey, don't get philosophical on me now. Let's start with bed."

Startled by the endearment, I started to say something, but she was in my arms all of a sudden, and there was nothing to do but kiss the woman.

We were just crossing the point of no return when a flash of lightning lit up the room like daylight. A split-second later, thunder shook the house. In my overheated state, I thought I saw two points of red light glittering in a dark corner but decided not to mention it.

"Close," I remarked.

"Very close. Let's go upstairs."

"Is that safe?"

"I hope not. Come on."

∞ ∞ ∞

It might have been an hour later; it might have been two or three hours. Who knew? The thunder and lightning had built into a violent storm that had knocked out the power at some point. What with one thing and another, we hadn't noticed. The electricity was back on now, because the time display on Cassie's alarm clock was flashing, but it didn't much matter.

She was asleep now, sprawled all over me. With one hand, I stroked her hair, getting a half-smile from her for that. I didn't know about her, but I'd just traveled to distant lands in bed and was starting to think better of fortune cookies.

"I could die now," I said softly.

The blonde head on my shoulder stirred. "You'd better not. I have first right of refusal on killing you."

I laughed. Same Cassie — thank God. "Thought you were asleep."

"Just resting. Thinking."

"About what?"

"All the things we have to talk about."

A very cold chill ran through me. Not much good could come of that. She was having second thoughts. The thrill of shattering the Commandments had worn off, and now she was starting to see that we couldn't be together, given our lives and our ...

She raised her head abruptly. "What's wrong?"

"Nothing."

"Don't you *dare* try that line on me. It's bad enough when men do it." In what little light there was, I saw a blue flash of anger in her eyes. "Your heart just jumped for no reason, and I want to know why."

"The talk thing," I said reluctantly. "I know what that usually means."

"Well, it *usually* just means we should talk. What did you think?"

Uncomfortable, I pulled the covers closer. "I don't know. Second thoughts? I don't blame you. I just —"

To my surprise — and annoyance — she started laughing.

"Something amusing?" I asked with a touch of ice.

"You." She bent down to kiss me. "You should know me better, Devvy. You're not getting rid of me *that* easily. Not after six years. Understand?"

Not really. But I smiled a little anyway.

"Good," she said and snuggled back down.

By reflex I stroked my fingertips down her bare side. "Do you want to talk now?"

"No. Keep doing that, will you?"

I did. She was very warm, and her softness felt good, all the curves starting to feel familiar.

"No one would believe this," she murmured. "The evil Devlin Kerry, petting someone."

"Evil?"

"Well, you can be the very devil when you want to be."

"I had private lessons." It was just a throwaway remark, but this time, I felt Cassie's heart lurch. "What's the matter?"

"I don't want to talk about her. Not right now."

"Fine by me." I went back to stroking her. "Cass?"

"What?"

"Monica didn't mean a thing. I love you."

She relaxed completely, and after a while, she fell asleep. But I lay awake for some time, wondering whether I'd just told her a lie.

Chapter Four

Sunday

I woke in a tangle of peach floral sheets in a shiny brass bed in a peach-and-white bedroom. Blinking in the sunlight, I tried to sort out where I was...and then recognized the jasmine notes of Cassie's perfume on the sheets. That brought last night back in a rush. Must have slept like the dead to wake up *that* far out of it.

I felt fantastic.

Trying not to whistle, which would be smug, I washed up in the peach-and-blue bath and then searched for my clothes. My shirt was missing, but it was bound to turn up somewhere, so I put on the blazer and the slacks and padded downstairs in bare feet.

Cassie was in the kitchen, drinking coffee and leafing through the Sunday paper. She smiled when I wandered in, and not quite as a joke, I put both hands over my heart in a show of admiration. She had on a kimono that I'd never seen before — nothing fancy, but flattering — and even with only traces of last night's makeup, she looked great. It figured.

Mindful of my new priorities, I kissed her good morning before I got coffee.

"I was going to wake you up in a few minutes," she said.

"Were you?"

"Mm-hmm. Care to know how?"

The first swallow of coffee almost went down the wrong way. "Care to show me?"

"Show yourself. Just push the button with the red arrow on it."

I followed her glance to a CD boom box on the counter and sighed. "If this is more *Golden Throats* ..."

"It's not. Red arrow."

Mistrustful, I pushed the button — and jumped back as a pulsing disco beat blasted out. "Hot Stuff" of all things. What was Cassie doing with Donna Summer CD's?

"Don't give me that look," she said, amused. "We saw *The Full Monty* together, remember?"

I remembered. We'd had so much fun that we both bought the video the following year. It had been a lot more fun in the theater, though; everybody had been chair-dancing, and a few people had even gotten up to dance in the aisles. The manager had tried to restore order at first, but he finally gave up and started dancing, too. He got a standing ovation.

The memory made me smile, and involuntarily, both feet started tapping. I caught myself just before the tapping turned into actual dancing and sneaked a look at Cassie. She'd seen. In fact, she was smirking.

"You know you want to," she said.

That damn song was starting to get to me. I hated disco, but there was no avoiding the need to keep time to this kind of thing. "Just between you and me?"

"Cross my heart."

I shook my head, knowing that I'd regret it later, but put the coffee mug down and gave in to the rhythm. It had been a while, but it came back. Cassie got up to lean against the counter and watch.

"Not bad," she remarked, "but this is the *Full Monty* soundtrack. I don't believe you've quite got the spirit of the thing. Do you really need all those clothes?"

"You're not serious."

"Well, you don't *have* to, of course. But if you *love* me ..."

I was going to regret this, all right, but I did love her. So I unbuttoned the top button of my blazer, flashed the lapel and raised an eyebrow at her.

"Oh, yeah. That's more like it. Are you wearing anything under that?"

"Couldn't find my shirt this morning," I replied, concentrating on my footwork on the way into a turn.

"I'm wearing it."

Startled, I tripped halfway through the spin. Cassie just laughed and took off her robe. All she had on was my shirt, mostly unbuttoned. It looked better on her.

"Don't stop," she ordered, moving with the beat herself now. When she got close enough, she unbuttoned the next button down on my blazer. "Your turn."

"It's Sunday morning," I said, unbuttoning her in return. "Everyone in town is getting ready for church, and you and I are doing *this*."

"You bet we are. Move your feet, sailor."

I gave up and let the music take its course.

∞ ∞ ∞

"We've got to stop having sex, Cass. It could lead to dancing."

"Well, at least now we know what disco is good for."

It had certainly been good for that. We were just now getting around to having breakfast, at 10:00 in the morning. If I looked over Cassie's left shoulder, I could see my shirt dangling from a potted tree, and it was best not to dwell on how that had happened.

"I thought we could just hang out today," she said. "Maybe go to the art museum or the mall or catch a movie. Something like that. What do you think?"

"Anything you want. I need to go home and change first, though." Trying to avoid seeing the shirt in the tree, I checked the outdoor thermometer on the bay window. "Looks like it's sweater weather."

"That reminds me — let's go shopping. I saw a sweater at Paul Harris the other day that just about matches your eyes."

I didn't quite know what to say to that, but it made me feel weirdly good.

"I thought for the longest time that your eyes were black," she said.

"Not too far off. An old boyfriend said they reminded him of motor oil after two thousand miles."

Cassie looked disgusted. "What a thing to say. That wasn't that Phil creep, was it?"

"Nope. That was Stu. Didn't I tell you about him?"

"I don't know if I want to know. How would you hook up with someone who knows what motor oil even *looks* like, anyway?"

"It was high school. He had a car. He was cute — for where I come from, anyway."

A moment of silence. "This conversation makes me feel very peculiar," she finally said.

"Why? You know I dated guys. In fact, up until a couple of months ago, you were always *pushing* them on me."

She sighed. "It made me feel better. God knows what I'd have done if you'd ever *let* me fix you up. I probably would've made it a double date and watched your boy like a hawk — and if he'd touched you, I'd have sawed his part off. It would've absolutely ruined *my* date's evening."

Now the silence was from my side of the table. "This would be one of the things we have to talk about," I said slowly. "You went out with everything but the kitchen sink and the Vienna Boys' Choir. You *also* weren't celibate."

She reached over to take my hand. "No, I wasn't. I'm human. Besides, I thought you were never going to feel the same way about me. But I talked a lot more than I did. *That* made me feel better, too." Gently, she rubbed the hand she was holding with the edge of her thumb. "Why? Did it bother you?"

"More than you know," I admitted. "I never knew why."

"I love you. I have for a long time. No one meant anything."

"It's all right if someone did, Cass. That was before."

Her grip tightened at that. "Nobody's that noble, Devvy, and I know for a fact that *you're* not. Knock it off. This is me, remember?"

"Impossible to forget." I had to smile against my will. "All right — I was jealous sometimes. Been there, rode the ride, bought the T-shirt. So let's just say we've had this conversation and drop it. Deal?"

"I wish we could. But we still have to talk about the witch sometime."

Very true. But not today. "Whenever you want, sweetheart. Now, suppose we ... what?"

"You just called me 'sweetheart.' "

Her expression was intent but unreadable. Wary, I ran back over what I'd just said. "Guess I did. It just slipped out. I don't have to —"

She cut me off with a kiss.

"Sweetheart," I repeated in the interest of experimenting with this phenomenon.

Another kiss.

"Baby duck?"

She laughed. "Nice try. I guess it meant the same thing, though. You can't really call your best friend 'honey' or 'sweetheart' or 'pookie' or —"

"Don't ever use that word on me," I warned. "*Are* you still my best friend, by the way?"

"Now more than ever." She put a friendly kiss on the bridge of my nose. "So did we decide on the mall?"

∞ ∞ ∞

You could set your watch by traffic patterns in Greenville, and weekday rush hours weren't the half of it. We had a day-care rush, a soccer-practice rush and even a Twelve Step rush, although nobody talked about that one. Sundays were just the same. Everyone went to church between 9:00 and 11:00, and then all the restaurants filled up. After that, it was on to the mall.

Cassie and I had fooled around (literally) so long that we didn't get to The Landing until 12:30, which meant we had to park in the back forty and walk. But it was a nice day, and it didn't matter anyway.

"The usual?" she asked as we crossed the ocean of asphalt. That meant Sharper Image, Pottery Barn, Sam Goody, Borders, Starbucks and then the little specialty shops. We'd done the circuit together any number of Sunday afternoons.

"Works for me. What about Nordstrom?"

"Next time. I'm fine on shoes for a while." She eyed my footwear critically. "So are you. Thank God you don't go around in Nikes. I got so sick of dating wannabe kids."

"Like them?"

We checked out the very young couple headed toward us, both wearing gaudy athletic shoes, jeans, sweatshirts and backward baseball caps. They were hanging all over each other like they'd just discovered sex, which maybe they had. As we passed, they scanned our attire — khakis, sweaters, serious purses, even my nice Munro ankle boots — and gave us looks of biting disdain.

"Ow," I muttered. "Guess we asked for that."

She smiled slightly. "That's not it. They think we're losers who can't get dates."

"This is The Landing," I growled, "not Noah's Ark."

"Maybe I'll have to hang all over you, just to show them."

Her tone was teasing, but I wasn't having any of it. "No showing anybody anything. No PDA's. I mean it."

"It might be just a little late for that," she said, laughing. "We've already made out in front of half a dozen people and a client, not to mention whoever's seen that videotape by now."

"That's different. That's the agency. Strangers are a whole other thing. They might think we're —"

The unspoken word went off like a bomb in the noisy parking lot. Cassie stopped walking a split second before I did.

"We do *not* look like Connie the Barbarian," she insisted.

"We don't have to. We've got a problem, Cass."

She looked around to see whether anyone was within earshot. No one was, but just to be safe, she drew me into a space between two parked SUV's. "We don't have any problem. I don't know that we're gay. I wasn't sure about you when you were with ... her, but I know *I'm* not."

"I'll remind you that you unzipped me with your *teeth* in the kitchen this morning. Not that I minded for a second. But if you're not sure about *me* ..."

"This is different. I'm not into girls. I'm just into *you*."

"It may have escaped your notice," I said, biting off the words, "but I'm a girl. I would have thought that of all the people on earth, *you'd* have seen enough anatomy by now to know the difference."

"You know what I mean," she snapped. "I love you, not your parts."

"You didn't seem to have a problem with them before. You were even saying something about giving my trainer a tip at Christmas. So if —"

"I said that?" She seemed to be honestly puzzled. "When did I say that? Honey, you're at least ten pounds underweight."

That ruined what was left of my good mood. Crossing my arms, I leaned back against one of the SUV's and scowled at her.

"I didn't mean it like that," she said, annoyed. "It looks good on you. Really. Most people would just look scrawny, but —"

"You might want to stop talking now, before you make me mad."

She leaned back against the other SUV, biting her lip in thought. "You're afraid to fight with me now, aren't you?"

"No. But this is *such* a stupid thing to fight about. We're supposed to be fighting about whether we're gay or not, and —"

"I know. That's why we're fighting about this instead," she said quietly.

That *was* why. All the anger drained out of me. "We don't have to do this right now."

"Of course not. We're here to shop."

I regarded her hopefully. "We could still argue. When we get to The Museum Company, anyway, and you start trying on Egyptian jewelry."

"You're still mad about that brooch," she said, brightening. "I don't care — I *like* it. It looks good with my navy blazer."

"It *looks* like a pair of Egyptian junior stewardess wings. I kept telling you to try the Venetian stuff, but no — you had to play Queen of the Nile. You're too blonde for that, Cass."

She was smiling all the way now. "Did you see that episode of 'Seinfeld' when Elaine dated a gay guy?"

As non sequiturs went, that one was world-class. "Probably. What does that have to do with your arrested taste in jewelry?"

"She said it was the best of both worlds: sex and shopping." Cassie crossed the small distance between us and put both her hands flat on my chest. "She was right."

I was just leaning forward, surroundings forgotten, when a shadow fell into our space. Both of us jumped. A stocky man about our age was making for one of the SUV's, shopping bags in both hands.

"Pardon," I said, stepping aside.

He gave us a hellfire's-too-good-for-some-people look and fumbled for his keys. Cassie motioned to me to get out of the man's way.

As I walked around the back of the vehicle, I noticed a Family Foundation decal in the back window, along with one of those "Proud Parent of an Honor Student" stickers. I was underwhelmed by this information, but still couldn't quite tear my attention away for some reason.

"Shopping, Devvy," Cassie prompted.

I squinted a bit in the sunlight and then saw it clearly in the back window: two points of red light, glowing behind the tinted glass.

She was back. I was sure of it now. The question was what she wanted — and when she was going to tell me.

"Hello?"

I would have to let Cassie know, of course. But not just now.

"Sorry," I said. "Coming."

Chapter Five

Monday

Monday morning I wore the new sunglasses to work. Cassie had found them at a kiosk at the mall and insisted that I buy them, which settled that. They were the wraparound kind, very fast-looking, like something Italian race-car drivers would wear, and they looked indescribably silly on me. But I wasn't up to trafficking with co-workers at the moment, and the sunglasses at least made eye contact impossible.

More to the point, Cassie and I had spent the night apart to make sure that we both got our space. It was the reasonable thing to do; it was the mature thing to do; it was the reason why I was in such a bad mood. Without a word to man, woman or beast, I swept through the lobby, took the stairs and made straight for my office. The idea was to not have to talk to anyone until the first meeting and maybe not ever again.

Unfortunately, Jack's path crossed mine. He took in the dark clothes, the black raincoat and the black shades, and laughed. "Which one are you? Heckle or Jeckle?"

"Don't be ridiculous. Crows don't wear sunglasses."

"Well, I doubt they'd wear *those*. But you're too big for a crow anyway. Maybe you're really a raven."

Everything stopped, including time. I'd had that very thought on that hot, hung-over morning in July when the world stopped making sense. There'd been a blood-red sky, with three black birds circling in it, and then Monica had landed. I hadn't known that yet, though. She'd been just a shadow in the dark, a flash of red in the rear-view mirror, a whisper in the night ...

Just like now. This was just like how it had started.

"Kerry?"

Startled, I jumped a little. "Sorry. What were you saying?"

"Forget it. It was a bird joke. You feeling okay?"

"You really want an answer?"

He shook his head. "No. Listen, I was looking for you anyway. I need to call a standup with your team in about an hour. We've got a new hire. She's going to sit in with us on the Tom's meeting, and I thought you should all do a meet-and-greet first."

The Tom's meeting. Damn, I'd forgotten about it. "Fine. But do I have to be at the meeting? I've got another —"

"There might be videotape," he said, grinning.

I shoved him aside with my attaché, hard, and stalked on down the hall.

∞ ∞ ∞

There is no such thing as a normal ad agency, but J/J/G was insane even for that business. Take the concept of teams. We'd once worked pretty much according to Hoyle, in that a team was a copywriter and an artist. Period. But then Jenner had gone to one of those Outward Bound-type weekends for business owners, and it had warped him even further. He'd come back from the woods with a glorious vision of Community, in which the creative staff worked in brotherhood with the Philistines of the business department, so we'd wound up with these damn teams. If one of us had a meeting now, all of us had a meeting, unless we had a good excuse, like being dead.

No one had died lately, which was why I was standing in Jack's office that morning in communion with two copywriters, an art director, an account executive and an account manager. At the moment, the account manager was secretly running a fingernail up and down my spine, and I was doing my best to look noncommittal.

Jack kept us waiting a while. When he finally showed, he was in high spirits, which always meant trouble. "My people. How good of you to come to me on such short notice. I want you all to meet someone. She's with Jenner right now, but she should be —" A soft knock interrupted him. "Yo!"

The door opened, and a beautiful woman walked in. She might have been a cover girl for one of the kinkier magazines that Kurt read: tall, thin, blonde, cruel, very minimally dressed. I was irresistibly reminded of a black-leather getup I'd seen on TV somewhere ... and bit my lip hard to block the thought. Not my type, whatever that was; not only that, but the blonde on her probably wasn't real. Something about her coloring didn't go with the hair color.

Guiltily, I glanced at Heather, who was a slightly different shade of redhead this week. The girl changed hair color like underwear. She always went with red, but she'd gone from Rita Hayworth to Howdy Doody more than once, and for one terrible week last March, she'd even been magenta — a hairdressing accident, but still painful to witness.

"Everyone, this is Vanessa," Jack said. "No last name; she's been a model. Vanessa, this is everyone."

She smiled, or at least changed the position of her lips a bit. There was something unnervingly feline about her expression. "Charmed, I'm sure. Do they have names, Mr. Harper?"

"I think I'll let them tell you themselves. We'll go around the room like small children. Who's first?"

Chip was always a gentleman, even though he was also always an account executive, so he started. As he spoke, I turned to see what was wrong with Cassie, who'd stopped torturing me the moment Vanessa walked in. She was staring at the woman as though she couldn't believe such things existed. When her turn came to introduce herself, all she said was, "Cassandra Wolfe," and not very nicely, either.

Cassie was rude only to her friends, so her tone surprised me. To make up for it, I tried to look friendly. "Devlin Kerry. I'm associate creative direc —"

"Director in charge of sex. Yes, I know." The woman's smile shifted slightly, making her expression even more feline. "Mr. Jenner had a great deal to say about you."

I felt Cassie grab the back of my sweater — the one she'd bought me the day before. Around the room, everyone else got very busy coughing and shuffling their feet.

"Mr. Jenner is a creative man," I said carefully.

The woman held her smile but didn't reply.

"I wonder, Jack," Cassie said, "whether you're going to let us in on what her job here is. Or did you want us to go around the room again and guess?"

Jack leaned back in his chair, hands clasped smugly behind his head. "Well, we haven't quite decided that part. Jenner thinks we'll start her off as his special assistant. Send her to client meetings, have her report on how we're doing, let her find her own niche. He thinks she'll be a good fit for this team down the road, so we're starting her with you people today. Do what you can to make her feel at home."

"Happy to be of service," Troy said to her with his very best smile.

Her black eyes flickered over him with a trace of amusement and then settled on Cassie for some reason. Sensing bad karma, I checked my watch. "We've got Tom Johnson in five minutes, Jack."

"I know. Somebody fetch him up from the lobby. They said he's been here for half an hour already."

Chip sighed. Trouble. "I'll go."

"I'll go with you," Vanessa said unexpectedly.

The look on his face was the look of a man who'd won the lottery on Christmas morning. I didn't like it. Cassie grabbed my sweater again and whispered, "I'll talk to him."

"You and me both," I whispered back.

We all watched Chip hold the door open for her, and as they left, Kurt exhaled sharply.

"Special assistant, is she?" he asked Jack.

"Very special." Jack's grin grew wider, which might have been painful, considering that his split lip hadn't quite healed yet. "I know something about her that you don't."

"I'll bet," Heather all but spat.

I could bet, too, but didn't really want to know. "Which conference room for the meeting?"

"B," Jack said. "Strange that you're not more interested in our new employee, Kerry. I would have thought that you would be."

"Why?"

"Oh, no reason. No reason." He had always been a bad liar, and he knew I knew it, because he turned the grin up a notch. Then he clapped a hand to his lip. "Ow! Damn!"

"Get stitches, you nimrod," I said to him and left the room.

∞ ∞ ∞

"A fat man in a Santa suit, on a *sleigh*," Heather complained as we went back to our offices after the client meeting. "Dev, honestly, I can write something better than that. Even *Kurt* can."

"I know you can. But it's what the client wants."

"But it's *stupid*!"

"I know."

Troy snorted. "You think *you* got the short end? I've got to find a reindeer on two days' notice. *And* a damn hibachi. Where am I supposed to get a hibachi this time of year?"

I felt their pain. Three meetings with this man, and we'd finally caved and agreed to what he wanted: Santa, grilling Tom's cocktail sausages during a rest stop on Christmas Eve. Heather would have to write copy that explained this bizarre situation; Troy would have to work with live animals and artificial snow. They would both be extremely unhappy, which meant they'd be in and out of my office, which meant I would have to start locking my door again. At least we'd talked the client out of TV. There wasn't time now anyway, and print was bad enough.

"I've had those sausages," I remarked, trying for a little positive spin. "Tom's catered an Ad Club party last year. They're not bad."

"Maybe I'll write that they're made out of reindeer," Heather grumbled.

"All right, Ebenezer. Point taken." I smiled at Cassie, who'd been unusually quiet. "Just do your best. I'll see what I can do about a little extra bonus at the end of the year. God knows you've earned it."

She muttered something about blood money and went into her

office, followed by Troy. No doubt they wanted to get started complaining about the project — a welcome sign of initiative on both their parts. Cassie and I continued on down the hall.

"Everything all right?" I asked.

"I don't know yet. What do you think of Vanessa?"

Was that all? Relieved, I pulled her over, out of traffic. "I think she's just a side effect Jenner's having from all that Viagra. And she's nowhere near your league."

"That's not it," she lied, "but thank you. What I meant was, do you trust her?"

"No. Something about her ... something's not right."

"Exactly. I'm keeping an eye on her just in case. I'll be keeping an eye on *you*, too."

I started laughing. "Cass, you're losing traction. She doesn't do a thing for me."

"I mean to keep it that way," she said grimly.

"Give me a little credit. I've got better taste than that. Wound up with you, didn't I?" I checked my watch again. "Look, I've got to hear audition tapes. How about lunch later?"

"Can't; I've got a client. After work?"

"Trainer at 6:00. Dinner? Say, 7:30?"

"Your place?"

"I'll order in," I promised. "I've got to go. Consider yourself kissed goodbye."

"Coward," she said, mussing my hair. Then she went her way, and I went mine. First, though, I watched her go. It was all right to do that now, and it *was* a nice sight.

∞ ∞ ∞

The day crawled. I kept busy, but my mind kept drifting and always to things that a decent person doesn't think about at work. Everyone knew what was going on, and they went all out to encourage it; I was forever getting pulled over to hear X-rated jokes or learn techniques from male masters of the art. Down in Video, where I'd gone to see the final cut of the Kester Mortuaries ad, J.B. insisted that I take his chair at the console. Then he reached over me to start the tape. It was, of course, the security-camera footage.

"Oops. Wrong button," he said between snorts of laughter.

I finally retreated to my office, even though I knew Kurt would have less trouble finding me that way. When he walked in, I mentally drew my sword. Cut off the head, after all, and the body dies.

"Filthy day," he said casually, settling into my guest chair without an invitation. "Drizzle and gray as far as the eye can see. It's not good writing weather. I can't get motivated."

"And ...?"

"Well, you're the boss. I thought maybe you knew some tricks that would motivate me."

"I filled out a request for termination for you this morning," I said to him.

He froze in mid-smirk, one end of his walrus mustache drooping weirdly. "You what?"

"It's already attached to e-mail to Jenner. All I have to do is send."

"But you can't do that, Dev. Is this about that tape? C'mon, it was a joke. I do stuff like that all the time." With a visible jerk, he got the mustache straight again, but his color was still bad. "I thought we were friends. I thought you'd get over it."

"You're already working the angles," I said with no particular expression. "You're thinking that this has to go through Jack, because I report to him, and you figure that Jack won't let me fire you. But you forget that Jack reports to Jenner."

Kurt considered that fact. "Jenner won't let you fire me either. He loved the tape. Hell, he's threatened to fire *you* a dozen times."

"You also forget why he doesn't."

I sat back and watched him fumble with the puzzle pieces. There was no hurry; he wasn't dumb; he'd get it soon enough.

"No," he finally said.

"Cassie trumps you, boy. He won't fire me as long as he thinks she'll quit if he does. Sex always wins. You thought you knew that, didn't you?"

"But she won't sleep with him. Especially not if she's g —"

"There's a backup card, too. That tape business might be illegal. Everyone in that room heard Jenner say it was *your* idea, so the average juror —"

He was on his feet now in a full-tilt panic. "Dev, I beg you not to do this. I've got a wife. We're going to have a baby ... someday. Where would I find another job?"

"There are other ad agencies in town."

"But they're not like this one."

"No. They're normal. Any other agency would have fired you two years ago."

Kurt just stared. It was true; everyone knew it, including him.

"I'm sorry, Dev," he said.

"Are you?"

"I didn't know you'd take it this way. It just didn't seem like that big a deal. I wasn't out to get you."

"Of course you were. You always are. But let's not talk about me right now. Let's talk about Cassie."

That caught him way off guard. "Cassie?"

"Playing games with me is bad, Kurt. I'm your boss, so that was way beyond stupid. But playing games with *her* is unforgivable. You owe her an apology."

"All right. I can do that. I owe her."

"A public apology," I continued. "In front of as many people as you can round up."

"Sure thing. No problem."

"Tomorrow would be good."

"Tomorrow? But I've got those Hairport auditions tomorrow with all the models. You prom —" He checked my expression and almost bit his tongue in half. "Tomorrow. You got it. I'll get right on it."

"Another thing."

"Anything, Dev. What can I do?"

"You owe Cassie some money. She would've bet on us getting together, too."

Kurt collapsed into the guest chair bonelessly. My guess was that sudden release of tension — any kind of tension — was too much for him.

"No more pools, Kurt."

He shook his head.

"No more jokes."

"Absolutely not," he agreed. "Never again. Thank you, Dev. I mean it. *Thank* you. I promise I'll —"

"One more thing."

"Name it. Shoot."

"What's the story with this Vanessa?"

It had been the right question, because some of the tension snapped back. "I don't know any story. What do you mean?"

"Attached to e-mail," I prompted. "One click, and —"

"She's bi."

"Bi what? Biracial? Bipolar? Bituminous?"

"Ha ha. Bisexual."

"There's more to it than that," I said.

"I don't know all of it. Honest. I think it's just coincidence. Jenner met her at some club over the weekend."

"And that's why Jack thought I would be interested in her?"

All the tension was back now. He squirmed in the chair as though I'd just switched on the current.

"Kurt?"

"That's all I know. Really, Dev. If something's up, I honestly don't know what it is."

It was a lie, of course, but I'd already had enough fun with him for one day. "You'll let me know the minute you find out. Don't try to pretend that you won't."

"Sure thing. Right away. I swear."

"Now get out of here before I change my mind."

It was all Kurt could do not to sprint to the door. When he got there, though, he paused. "Boss?"

"Subordinate?"

"Thanks."

"Remember this," I said to him. "Close the door behind you."

He did. Then it was my turn to collapse. There was a request-for-termination form somewhere on the J/J/G server, and I'd have to find it in case somebody asked, but right now, I just wanted to enjoy the victory.

The better to enjoy it, I put the *Top Gun* soundtrack in the Discman and cranked up the volume — another guilty pleasure that was none of anyone's business. Not even Cassie knew I had this CD.

Halfway through "Danger Zone," I felt someone walk in and swiveled around to see who the problem was now.

She leaned over the desk to lift off my headphones, a mocking little smile on her lips.

"Hello, Devlin," Monica said.

Chapter Six

Monday Night

By the time Cassie got to the condo, right at 7:30, I was almost calm enough to hold a wineglass steady. A good thing, too, because she'd brought wine.

"We had this at the Midsummer Festival," she said as she poured. "I think it was at the Mezzaluna tent. If I remember right, you really liked it. You had a little much of it, anyway."

No argument there. For reasons that were no longer clear, I'd wound up lying on the lawn near the jazz stage, contemplating the moon. After a loud lecture about my conduct for the benefit of passersby, she lay down next to me.

"Look at that moon," I'd said. "It's beautiful. If I were drunk, I'd say it's romantic."

"You're very drunk, and it *is* romantic. A person could fall in love under a moon like that."

"But there are golf balls on it now, Cass. *Golf* balls. And American flags."

She'd been silent for a while. I'd thought she was coming up with her own list of space junk.

"I hope you fall in love with someone just like you someday," she'd finally said — and gotten up and walked away.

What I didn't know then. Worse, what I didn't know now.

"Cheers." Cassie clinked her glass against mine. "God, what a day. Wall-to-wall clients. I went home after work and soaked in the tub for an hour, just to get the day off me. How was yours?"

"Interesting."

"Uh-oh." Laughing, she reached over to take my hand. "Then we won't talk about it right now. Dinner looks great, by the way. I was just in the mood for Greek. Did you get baklava, too?"

"What's the point of having Greek food if you don't have baklava?"

"I adore you."

"I hope you mean that. I saw Monica today."

Cassie was good when she wanted to be. Her expression didn't change. "Monica who?"

Raising the hand that she was holding, I kissed hers and folded my other hand around it.

She sighed. "Monica. I should have known. That explains it. She's the red eyes I've been seeing, isn't she?"

All the alarm bells in the firehouse started clanging. "*You've* been seeing?"

"A couple of times. Saturday night, during that storm —"

"And in the back of that van at the mall yesterday," I added.

She almost withdrew her hand. "You didn't tell me."

"You didn't tell me, either."

"You saw it both times?"

"Both times. And all of her this afternoon."

"Damn."

"Exactly," I said.

We sat in silence for a minute.

"Devvy?"

"Sweetheart?"

"Don't 'sweetheart' me right now. What did you mean when you said you saw all of her?"

I pulled both hands away from hers. "What kind of question is that?"

"A question that I have every right to ask. If you ever want to see all of *me* again ..."

"She was all there — that's what I meant. More than just the eyes. She had that black dress on, if that's what you wanted to know." A little annoyed, I scowled at her. "Nothing happened. She scared me stupid, and then she disappeared. Nothing was *going* to happen, anyway. Don't you trust me?"

"I trust you. But you can't trust her."

"*There's* a news flash."

"I don't understand why you didn't tell me about her right from the start. You were acting really weird, even for you, so I knew something was up."

"You wouldn't have believed me if I *had* told you at the start. You didn't even believe it the first time you saw her. Besides, what could you have done?"

"What I did at the Halloween party."

"What — out yourself?"

"That was all she ever wanted, Devvy. First you and then me. It was that simple."

I watched her narrowly, thinking. "What was your deal with her?"

"Nothing much. She said she'd leave you alone if I took over for her. She *has* left you alone, hasn't she?"

"That way, yes. But something's not right here. There's got to be more to it than that."

"That's what she said."

"She lies," I reminded her. "She's a demon."

"Witch."

"*Cassie ...*"

She leaned into the candlelight and took my face in her hands. "Whatever she is, she's already got her deal. She's not getting any more out of either of us. We won't let her. Understand?"

"I hope you're right."

"So do I," she admitted and kissed me. "Could we have dinner now? I'm starving."

∞ ∞ ∞

We barely finished dinner, much less made it upstairs. It was still raining out, and Cassie decided that she wanted a fire, so I made one. Then she wanted the lights off, so I saw to that. As for what she wanted after *that* ...

"Now I want baklava," she said, wrapped in my arms and the couch throw.

"I don't think I can move just yet."

She looked up and brushed damp hair out of my eyes. "I don't want you to go anywhere. I want the baklava to come to me."

"You learned all the physics you know from 'Star Trek,' didn't you?"

"For someone who can't move, your lips seem to be working just fine." Snuggling closer, she pulled my arms tighter around her. I could still feel a light film of sweat on her body. "Keep me warm. A person shouldn't get chilled after a workout like that."

Truer words were never spoken.

"Can you walk yet?" she asked after a few seconds.

Exasperated, I pushed her away a little. "What *is* it with you wanting everything at the same time tonight? Do you want this or not?"

"Something's wrong," she mused. "Sex is supposed to be relaxing. Why don't we try that again and see what your problem is?"

There was no good way to respond to that, so I kept quiet.

Cassie laughed. "Oh, all right, I'll play nice. Forget I said anything."

That, I could do and did. We lay like that for a while, her fingers tracing light patterns on my skin. Slowly, I relaxed, lulled by the fire, the rain on the roof and Cassie's touch.

"That's better," she said. "Much, much better. You're getting sleepy. Very, very sleepy. Now, when I count to ten, you will get up ... and bring me baklava."

Without a word, I dumped her on the carpet. She landed sputtering but unhurt. Then I got up off the couch and back into my clothes.

Cassie watched, bemused, from the carpet, still wrapped in the couch throw. "Espresso would be nice, too."

"Remind me again why I'm with you," I said, zipping up.

She got up and came over to remind me. What I'd told Kurt that afternoon had been only half the truth; Cassie trumped *me*, too.

Then she gave me a little shove in the direction of the kitchen. "I'll be in to help. I'm just going to run up to the good bath."

"Careful. The medicine cabinet in that one's got a broken mirror. I haven't had a chance to get it fixed yet."

"I don't need a mirror for this," she said dryly.

I smiled after her as she went up the stairs. How all this had happened was still pretty much a mystery, but it was probably best not to think — just to close my eyes and hold on tight for the ride.

Flipping on the kitchen lights, I got the espresso going and started searching for the cups. I very seldom made espresso — the machine had been a Christmas present, and to be honest, I was a little afraid of it — so the paraphernalia that went with it was never right at hand.

The cups and the little spoons finally turned up in a cabinet behind the green tea and the flavored vinegars. While I inspected them for dust, the phone rang.

"Go ahead," Cassie said on her way back through the living room.

Shrugging, I picked up the wall phone. "Hello?"

"Hey, Kerry. How's non-celibacy treating you?"

"Make it fast, Walt," I snapped.

Cassie rolled her eyes in sympathy and crossed behind me.

"Won't take a second," he said. "I just saw something amazing on TV, and I had to call and share it with you."

"Define 'amazing.' "

"Well, it really can't be defined — it kind of has to be *seen*. Is Cassie there?"

"Are you here?" I asked her, loud enough for him to hear.

"No," she said. "Get bent, Walt."

I got back on the phone. "She says she's not, and you should —"

"Yeah, yeah, yeah. You want to hear this, or you want me to hang up?"

A warm hand turned my face its way and popped a piece of baklava into my mouth. Great — the second-worst jerk at J/J/G was on the phone looking for trouble, and there was a troublemaking blonde in my kitchen, wearing only a couch throw. It took a second to swallow and collect my wits again.

"Kerry?" Walt asked.

"Sorry. Now, just what is it that you're so hot to tell me?"

"Well, it's like this. I just saw the Rumours spot on Channel 10, and —"

"Impossible. We bought late-night cable. That slot on 10 should be ... what?" Frowning, I checked the time display on the microwave. "That'd be 'Ally McBeal.' The client couldn't even have afforded it. And what are *you* doing watching that show anyway?"

"I'm telling you, Kerry, I saw the spot. And that's not *all* I saw."

I didn't like his tone; he was building up to something bad. "Really? So what else *did* you see? Did Ally finally get her skirt so short that you saw London and France?"

Cassie, who'd been licking honey off her fingers, frowned and pressed up close to the phone to hear what was going on.

"I'm still talking about the ad. Remember that part the lawyers made you keep re-cutting?"

Every second of it. Every inch of those miles of tape. "Out with it, Walt."

"I really think you need to see it for yourself. Let me surf a second, and ... hey, whaddya know? There it is again!"

"What channel?"

"Channel 5. It just started."

"Would you mind turning on Channel 5?" I asked Cassie.

Puzzled, she let go and went back to the living room.

"She's getting it," I said to him. "We didn't buy *this* slot, either, so we're going to check your story and then call the paramedics. I really think you've lost —"

"Oh, God," I heard Cassie say.

I turned, startled, to check the TV. It was the Rumours ad, all right. The second segment was just ending, and the kiss was about to begin.

"Kerry? You still there?" Walt asked.

I started to answer — but then I saw Cassie and myself on the TV screen, and the phone dropped out of my hand.

Chapter Seven

Cassie recovered *first*. She switched off the TV and marched back to the kitchen, looking determined. First, she hung up the phone, which was still dangling by its cord a few inches off the floor. Then she poked a finger into my chest.

"We didn't see that," she informed me.

"No," I agreed.

"It was the wine."

"No question."

"I'll just change, and then we'll have coffee."

"Perfect."

She gave me one last poke for emphasis and retreated to find her clothes. While she dressed, I checked the espresso, wondering whether it was possible to add more caffeine at this stage of the brew cycle. Then things started beeping and ringing and buzzing all over the place — my phone again, her cell phone, my PowerBook, her pager. My pager was probably going off, too, but there was no way to know for sure; I kept it in the bottom drawer of a file cabinet at the office.

"Don't answer any of that," she said, buttoning her sweater. "You're not home, and I'm not here."

"So you want to go all the way with the denial thing, do you?"

"It's not denial. Just a delay. Are *you* ready to deal with them right now?"

After a few seconds' thought, I unplugged the kitchen phone. Then, methodically, I went through the condo, unplugging and turning things off. Cassie, having turned off her cell phone and pager, went around to all the ground-floor doors and windows, making sure that they were locked.

When I came back downstairs, all the lights were off again. She was lounging on the couch, bare feet on the coffee table, calmly sipping espresso.

"We just bunkered ourselves in against our friends," I remarked. "There's got to be something wrong with that."

"Really? What?"

I considered briefly. "Never mind."

She patted the place next to her, and I took it, along with the other cup of espresso and a piece of baklava. In companionable quiet — and very deep denial — we watched the fire. After a while, I gave that up and just watched her.

She was well worth watching. She wasn't wearing anything suggestive — just a red button-front sweater and a pair of faded jeans — but it all fit like a million bucks, and the degree to which she'd left the sweater unbuttoned suggested many things to me. In the firelight, her hair had subtle red highlights that I'd never noticed before; they went well with the sweater and the jewelry. Cassie was the kind of woman who would wear earrings and a couple of bangle bracelets to clean the garage, which had always been a point of contention between us. Except for watches, I didn't wear much jewelry, and she thought that was a serious character flaw. Only the fact that I liked shoes redeemed me in her eyes.

With some amusement, I glanced at one of the bracelets on her right wrist — a Chinese design, which I'd bought her at The Museum Company the day before to make up for what I'd said about her Egyptian junior stewardess brooch. (I still meant every word of it, though.)

Cassie finally felt my attention, smiled and curled up against me like a cat. Feeling better already, I pulled her closer and checked the fire again. It would need another log before long if we were going to stay downstairs a while. My hope was that we wouldn't.

Not that I should have been thinking about that just then. We were in trouble; we needed a plan. Without a plan, we'd be walking into a wolf pack tomorrow without weapons. But tomorrow was still a while off. And although the woman next to me was part of the problem, she was also an excellent solution.

There might be a perfectly logical explanation for what had happened anyway. J.B. had a copy of the security-camera tape; he might have cut it into a copy of the Rumours commercial for the Christmas-party reel. Maybe there were copies of *that* going around already, and maybe those copies had fallen into the wrong hands, by mistake or design. A new account executive might have delivered the wrong tapes to the broadcast stations. Or maybe Jack and Kurt had found somebody who could hack the stations' signals. It was possible — barely. But ...

"Stop thinking about it," Cassie said.

"What makes you think I'm thinking?"

"When are you ever not?" She drew back just enough to lock her eyes with mine. "Let's have it, Devvy. Get it out of your system. You talk in your sleep, and I only want to hear *good* things tonight."

"I talk in my sleep?"

She gave me the Get On With It look.

"All right, fine. I was just trying to figure out how it could have happened."

"And ...?"

I told her. She shook her head. "Too complicated."

"It's the only way it makes sense," I protested.

"Stop trying to make things make sense. I hate it when you do that."

"You have a better explanation?"

"She's *your* demon. If you can explain her, go right ahead."

Silence. Cassie was right; this was Monica's doing, and we were never going to be able to explain it. Damn.

"Your deal with her," I said. "When you said you'd take over for her, exactly what did you agree to?"

"To make sure you weren't celibate, for one thing. *That's* been a hardship." She kissed me, lingering. "Honey."

"What?"

"No, I mean you've got a little right there." Leaning in again, she licked my lips. Every nerve in my body thwanged. This was definitely ...

... distracting. "One thing at a time, Cass. What else did she tell you?"

She sighed. "This conversation is going to put me right out of the mood."

"I'll put you back in it later. Promise. Now, what she did say?"

"Oh, all *right*. She told me not to let you change your mind. I said I was good at that. Then she laughed." Cassie mock-shuddered. "It sounded like a million cats in heat. Anyway ..."

"That'll be the important part," I said grimly. "After she laughed."

"Important? Please. She just said once we were both out, we had to stay out. That stands to reason, right? So I said, 'Fine.' That was that. Satisfied?"

I went back over it a couple of times. We were out; we had to stay out. Neither of us had ever been in any closet, exactly, but the secret was out, and as for staying out, it was doing a nice job of that on its own. So we'd given her the bargain she wanted, unless ...

Unless she meant "out" a whole different way — unless she meant *way* out, beyond the agency. Which was out of the question.

She knew that, of course. *Now* things made sense. Monica had put that tape on TV to out us in public ... and to nail the closet door shut behind us.

"Honey?"

Still thinking, I wiped my mouth absently.

"I mean you this time. What's wrong?"

"She has us, Cassie."

"No, she doesn't. She's just trying to scare us. I don't think —"

"She meant we had to advertise. We can't do that, and she knows it. *That's* why she made a deal with you. She knew she'd win. She's got us."

Cassie regarded me sharply. "She hasn't got us yet."

"Fine. Tell that to everyone you know who watched TV tonight. Tell it to the first client who recognizes you — or asks you out. Or the first old boyfriend you run into. What are you going to say? 'Sorry, but I just went gay all of a sudden, just like *that*. It was that damn Tinky Winky. The little purple bastard jumped off a store display and sucked my blood. It was awful. Just aw —' "

"If that were funny, I'd tell you to stop being funny," she said with a bit of asperity. "This isn't about the gay thing. It's about you and me."

"We *are* the gay thing now. The plumbing matches. If you want to call a doctor to confirm it, we can do that, but I'm telling you —"

"Dammit, Devvy, I am *not* getting labeled like that. I don't even *like* lavender. It's a bad color for me."

"Cassie," I said flatly. "Listen to me. We're poster children for diversity now, whether we want to be or not. We can play word games all you want, but as long as we're together, we *are* gay."

"I don't like it," she muttered.

"I don't either. But there it is."

Silence again, for so long that I almost checked her pulse.

"Maybe one rainbow," she finally said.

"What?"

"I could live with one rainbow on something. A very small pin, maybe, or a key chain." She kept a straight face but poked me in the ribs to let me know she was joking.

"We could have T-shirts made," I suggested, "that both say 'HERS.' "

"As long as they're not lavender. How about hot pink?"

"Hate it. What about black?"

"You already wear too much black. Remind me to do something about your wardrobe soon. How about red?"

"Looks better on you. Navy?"

"*That* looks better on *you*." She fingered the soft cotton of my navy sweater. "It looks good off you, too. Why don't we go upstairs?"

I tried to look offended. "Are you suggesting that we do something gay?"

With a wicked glint in her blue eyes, she put her arms around me and whispered something. Before the shock of the words wore off, she blew lightly in my ear. My entire nervous system shorted out on the spot.

"You are a very evil person," I complained.

She laughed and pulled me upstairs behind her.

∞ ∞ ∞

While the fire downstairs burned out, we lit another one upstairs. It was a wonder that the sheets didn't go up in flames. Cassie was definitely back in the mood, and I got a little carried away myself. All this went on for a while. Not bad for a Monday night in Greenville, even for consenting adults in private.

What we didn't know, while we were consenting that night, was that our private lives were already over.

Chapter Eight

Tuesday, 2:00 a.m.

Where she'd come from, I didn't know, but this gorgeous, green-eyed blonde had more curves than a Grecian urn, and she was dying to dance. Ever since she'd found out that dancing wasn't allowed, she'd wanted to do it more than anything. Was I interested?

Yes. I was human, with red blood and working parts. Besides, she looked a bit like Cassie, so where was the harm? I smiled and held out a hand to her. Her fingers folded into my grip as though they were made for it. Then she closed all the space left between us. Even though she was a few inches shorter, she was a perfect fit, and every cell of my body suddenly remembered hers. We'd done this before — this, among other things. I was absolutely certain of that.

"Dance," she prompted.

"Who leads?" I asked.

"Who cares?"

Excellent point. We tried it both ways and then compromised, more or less swaying together in place. That was perfect.

"They'll be coming for us soon," she said, tilting her head back just enough to look into my eyes. "We'll have to fight. Will you?"

"Till hell freezes," I promised her.

A half-smile flickered on her lips. "And then we'll fight on the ice?"

"That would be hockey."

"That's all right," she said. "I know how to use a big stick."

At which point I woke up, absolutely furious. Whatever that wine was, I was never touching it again.

Cassie, disturbed by the movement, stirred a bit in her sleep. Careful not to wake her, I smoothed her hair and tried to relax again. Everything was all right; no one was coming for us; it was too early in the season for ice, even in hell.

But damn, that dream had felt real ... and familiar. Something about her had been Cassie, in a way that I couldn't define, to the point that I wondered what *she* was dreaming right now.

Then again, maybe I'd finally snapped, and no wonder — the human psyche probably wasn't wired to handle a demon, an advertising career and Cassandra Wolfe all at the same time. In the morning, I'd have to call Dr. Shapiro. Maybe she could check me in somewhere for a nice long rest before anyone got hurt.

Better yet, I'd call a travel agent; Cassie could use a rest, too. A week at the beach still sounded good, and if we went to Florida, we could stop by New Orleans on the way back. The great thing about that town — besides Cajun food, jazz and voodoo — was license. We could probably go around the Quarter in fake antlers, if we wanted, and nobody would blink.

Staring absently at the ceiling fan, I started mapping the Quarter in my head, trying to remember where everything was. I was halfway down the Rue Decatur when the fan blades started to turn.

At first, I was merely puzzled. The fan had been off all night. It was still raining, but there'd been no lightning to fool with the electricity. The condo's wiring was a little touchy sometimes, though, so I made a mental note to call the landlord. Meanwhile, it wouldn't hurt to let the fan run.

All right. Decatur Street. That brewpub was across the street from —

Jesus, what was *that*?

No, I knew what it was; the question was *why* it was. I'd played that Cowboy Junkies CD a few days ago, but I always put discs back in their jewel cases, and the CD player had been off since the weekend. But even if I'd been careless enough to leave the disc in the player and the player on, why would a track start anywhere but the start?

"Devvy?" Cassie murmured.

Trying to get my heartbeat down so as not to alarm her, I kissed the top of her head. "Hmm?"

"What is that?"

" 'Blue Guitar.' Go back to sleep."

In the very next instant, everything in the condo came on: lights, major appliances, gadgets and widgets and gizmos of all kinds. Cassie shot bolt upright. I did my best to keep a secure hold on her, just in case.

"What *is* that?" she asked again.

"I don't know. But I think we've got company, Cass."

She stared at me, not quite comprehending. "That's my pager going off downstairs. I took the battery out."

"Can't be, if you took the battery out. It might be —"

The phone rang.

"I thought you unplugged the phones," she said.

"Stay here," I warned, grabbing my robe and going around the bed. Sure enough, the phone was still unplugged, but it was ringing, and there was something in the Caller ID panel. I leaned over to check. The display read 7734.

"What is it, Devvy?"

"I don't know. Not a phone number."

Cassie got her own robe off the footboard and pressed up behind me, looking at the display around my shoulder. Then she snorted.

"What?"

"It's an old joke. Read it upside down."

Upside down? I tried to visualize it ... and then saw. "Damn."

"She's back," Cassie said.

"That was my guess."

"What do you suppose she wants?"

"Only one way to find out." Reluctantly, I picked up the phone. "Monica?"

Her laughter purred in my ear. "Did I scare you?"

"No. Where are you?"

"Downstairs. You're lying about not being scared, by the way. Did you like the Caller ID trick?"

"No. What do you want?"

"What do *you* want?"

"Don't answer questions with questions," I said testily. "I hate when people do that. You're not technically 'people,' but —"

"Neither were you, *technically*, until I showed up. You really should thank me for it, you know."

"Hang up," Cassie advised.

Monica laughed again. "Don't you want to hear my offer first?"

I turned to Cassie. "Do we want to hear her offer first?"

Evidently not; she took the phone out of my hand and banged it down.

"That won't work," I remarked.

"If she's going to haunt us, the least she can do is haunt us in person. I hate a rude witch."

"Demon," Monica said.

We spun around. Monica was lounging on the bed, looking very much at home. In fact, she was wearing the black silk robe that matched mine instead of her usual black gown — that, and a rather proprietary air.

"We'll have to burn those sheets now," Cassie muttered.

"She's a fighter," Monica said approvingly. "You'll need that. You're going to have trouble."

"What do you want?" I demanded.

"What *you* want. Catch."

My reflexes were working just fast enough to make the catch. "Fortune cookies?"

Cassie frowned. "I hate those things."

"You'll like these," Monica assured her. "Go on. Open them."

Against my better judgment, I did, and handed one strip to Cassie.

"I'll bet it says 'Surrender Dorothy,' " she said.

" In bed," I added.

Cassie smiled knowingly. "Well —"

"Later," Monica snapped. "Read them."

We unfolded the fortunes and compared them. They both said, "Remember nothing."

"Meaning what?" I asked.

"Meaning that I'm prepared to offer you an out ... so to speak. I can make that tape go away. All of it. Including your television debut last night."

"That was your fault in the first place. That'd be like asking the train that ran over you to do it again, only faster. What are you up to?"

She tried to look innocent, or at least as innocent as someone with fangs could. "Very suspicious, Devlin. I come here in good faith."

"That'd be a first," Cassie grumbled.

Monica shot her a look that I didn't like, so I got physically between them. "Let's get this over with. Let's hear the deal."

With a bad word, Cassie pulled me back. "Have you lost your mind?"

"Very likely," I admitted. "All right, Monica — let's have it. And make it short. It's 2:00 in the morning."

She made it short. The deal was this: She would undo everything she'd done since the night we met, and no one would remember any of it. There'd be nothing to explain, nothing to defend, nothing to keep secret. For all practical purposes, we'd go back to normal. We'd *be* normal ... as far as anyone knew. Monica knew that normal mattered.

The catch was this: Cassie and I wouldn't remember either.

"No deal," Cassie said instantly.

"Not so fast," Monica said. "Think it over. You have no idea what you're in for."

"I *know* what I'm in for."

For some reason, Monica found that amusing. "It can get worse. I could visit a few other people before morning. They might wake up with some very interesting ideas."

"Don't waste your time. Jenner doesn't have two brain cells to rub together, much less to start an idea with."

"I *like* vacuums. Nature abhors them, but I've always found use for them. And your Mr. Jenner is as vacant as Macy's on Thanksgiving morning."

Caught off guard, I laughed. Cassie gave me a sharp nudge.

"Sorry," I said and then turned to Monica. "We're not interested in any deal. We'll take our chances."

"You'll regret this," she warned.

"Maybe. But tell me something. Why would you make this offer in the first place?"

To my surprise, she smiled without malice. "For old times' sake. To save you some pain. Call me a sentimental fool."

"Speaking of pain," Cassie said, "I don't know whether you bleed, but if you're not gone in ten seconds ..."

Her smile changed slightly. "Devlin may have been a bad influence on you."

"The worst. Now get out of here."

"I could make you fat," Monica said, a devilish glint in her eye. "Or flat in certain places. I could even —"

I'd heard all I cared to. "*Enough*. Both of you."

They both fell silent and glared at me, equally annoyed. Interesting.

"Let's call it a night. We've got a long day tomorrow, so let yourself out, Monica. Turn the lights off again when you leave, if you don't mind."

"You haven't said yes to my offer, Devlin."

"No, because the answer is no. Thank you, but no."

"You'll regret this," she repeated. "But I'll leave you an out in case you change your mind. If either of you wants to accept, all you have to do is say so. I'll hear you."

"Good night, Monica," I said.

She shook her head, and then she was gone. All the strangeness went with her, and we were standing in a dark, quiet bedroom with a ceiling fan slowing to a stop.

"It was bad enough dating divorced daddies," Cassie said conversationally. "Then I had to go and get involved with someone who has a demon."

"And *I* had to go and get involved with someone who talks back to her. C'mere."

She held the kiss longer than I meant it to last — so long, in fact, that we almost fused. Then she tilted her head back just enough to look in my eyes. She was almost as tall as me, but suddenly, she felt a bit smaller.

"Have you ever had blue eyes and a sword?" she asked.

"Not to my knowledge. What kind of question is that?"

"I don't know. I was having the strangest dream, and you just reminded me of it."

Carefully, I held her off a bit to get a better look at her. It was dark in the room except for some spillover light from the streetlamps, so I couldn't be sure. But for a second, I would have sworn that her eyes were green.

"What?" she asked.

"Were we dancing in this dream?"

"Not exactly. It was against the law or something." Now she was sizing me up. "You looked different, but it was you."

"It was probably one of Monica's tricks. She works that way sometimes. She used to give me the same dream every night for weeks."

"Well, this one, I'll take. You were a lot more aggressive. I liked it."

My eyebrows shot up.

"It was kind of sexy," she continued.

I thought about it for a minute. "Blue eyes and a sword, huh?"

"You won't need the sword right now," Cassie said, "and I suggest that you close your eyes."

Chapter Nine

Tuesday

Sunglasses and attitude got me to my office without challenge in the morning. I was counting on the attitude — and a thermos of espresso from home — to get me through the day. Cassie had counseled courage in the form of stonewalling. Nobody would know for sure what had happened, she said, and what nobody knew wouldn't hurt us. Besides, she reminded me, J/J/G was full of squidbrains who were lucky to remember their own names.

True enough. But no sooner did I walk through the door than my local line buzzed. It was Jenner's admin, Sanchez, with the news that at least one squidbrain had remembered last night and that he wanted to see Cassie and me right away.

Cassie was out on client calls all morning, so that left me. Filling the biggest mug in the office with espresso, I went upstairs to face whatever there was to face.

Sanchez was on the phone when I got to Jenner's suite, looking as though she'd been on the phone for days, and it wasn't even 9:15 yet. Genuinely feeling her pain, I put a hand on her shoulder in passing. She smiled, but wanly.

Drawing a long breath, I knocked on Jenner's closed door.

"If that's another lawyer," I heard him roar, "wring his balls!"

"Yes, sir," Jack said. Then he shouted at the door, "Who is it?"

"Not a lawyer!" I shouted back.

The door flew open. "About time," Jack growled. "Where in hell have you been? Why isn't Wolfe with you?"

"She left me for a palomino. The weird part is, it was a girl."

He didn't even smirk.

"Well, dammit, asking a question like that is just asking for trouble. Now, am I supposed to come in?"

"Kerry's here, sir," he called over his shoulder.

"Where's Miss Wolfe?" Jenner asked.

"I don't know. Should I ask her?"

"Ask who?"

"Kerry."

"I thought you said Derry was here."

"She is, sir. Her name's Kerry."

"Kerry who?"

A scene from a Marx Brothers movie flashed through my mind: *You can't fool me. There ain't no sanity clause.* Wearily, I leaned against the doorjamb and waited.

"We could have her come in," Jack said, "and see if the sight of her jogs your memory."

"I don't want to be jogged. I want to see Miss Wolfe and Derry."

"Brain-damaged mothering sonuvabitch," Jack muttered, standing aside to let me in the office.

Jenner was pacing the carpet like a pinstriped tiger, looking crazier even than usual. When he spotted me, he stopped pacing long enough to point a finger. "Derry, you're late."

"Not very, sir. It's only seven aft —"

"Where's Miss Wolfe?"

What was I — her keeper? "Working, sir. She had some clients to see."

"Page her again, Miss Sanchez!" Jenner yelled through the open door. Promptly, Jack closed it again.

I shook my head and then noticed Vanessa parked on Jenner's couch, looking right at home. Very likely she was. Her skirt was hiked halfway to Nome, at any rate, and she seemed not to care who saw what. It was a flip of the coin whether she'd been in the process of dressing or undressing when all this commotion had started.

She gave me a sly smile, as though she knew something that she wanted to tell, and patted the couch cushion next to her. As coldly as possible, I turned away.

"We'll start without her, then," Jenner said. "We have no choice. Look at that, Derry."

"Look at what, sir?"

He pointed at something on his desk. It could have been anything — the stuffed baby alligator, the Malay dagger, the temple bell ...

Jack saw the dilemma. "Here. Take my copy." He handed me the Metro section of that day's *Herald*, folded over and open to an inside page. "Did you see this?"

"Didn't have time to read the paper this morning. What am I looking at?"

"It's right in front of you."

"What — the jewelry ad? That's not our account."

"Right above it."

I scanned up.

Foundation to Fight Bad Ads
HERALD STAFF REPORT

> Saying there is "a moral crisis in our living rooms," the Family Foundation is announcing a campaign against indecent advertising in the metroplex area.
>
> Family Foundation Chairman Howard Abner said the group intends targeting local advertising agencies that "expose our young people to degeneracy, deviancy and depravity." He said two of the worst examples are J/J/G Advertising and Ad House, known for their "edgy," sexually suggestive advertisements.
>
> A boycott of all of the clients of these agencies is possible, he said.
>
> The foundation will hold a press conference about this matter Wednesday morning at 10:00 at its headquarters, located at 11911 S. 115th St. in Greenville. The general public is invited to attend.
>
> Persons wanting information can call the foundation's offices at 555-1050.

"Well?" Jenner demanded.

"Terrible writing," I said seriously.

Overcome by some great emotion, Jenner pointed a trembling finger at Jack. Then he started pacing again.

"Mr. Jenner, I don't see the problem," I said. "They've targeted us before. In fact, you personally have *tried* to get them to target us, for the publicity. Remember when you wanted to send them the work tape of Rumours? And speaking of Rumours —"

Jenner wheeled around, one foot still in the air. "Ha!"

"Ha, sir?"

"I'll translate," Jack said impatiently, snatching the paper back. "This story is way behind the curve now. That press conference got called before the little accident with that spot last night. *Before* you and Wolfe became prime-time TV stars."

We were down to it now. For courage, I swallowed most of the contents of my mug — and remembered a split-second too late that it was espresso, not regular coffee. The room began to vibrate slightly as all that caffeine slammed into my system.

Then Cassie stormed into the office, coat still on, car keys still out and fire in her eyes.

"The next time I get that many pages in fifteen minutes," she said direly, "I'm going to get a great big stick and start taking people down with it. The client is *not* happy. Why am I here?"

If Jenner had heard a word of what she'd said, he heard it only as sound. He'd stopped pacing and was openly studying her legs with a wild gleam in his eyes.

Cassie's temper rose visibly. "I had to agree to have lunch with the client. I *also* had to reschedule two other appointments. This trashes my day. What did I get called back here for?"

Jack handed her the paper and told her the story. Meanwhile, I took a seat on one armrest of the couch — the one farthest from Vanessa. The room was still vibrating, and what I really wanted to do was lie down, but there was always the carpet if matters got desperate.

"So?" Cassie asked when Jack finished.

"So you and Kerry were all over TV last night, and that puts us in a really bad position."

"Puts *you* in a bad position?"

"Vis-à-vis Howard Abner."

She told him, using very definite language, what he could do vis-à-vis Howard Abner, the Family Foundation, every client on J/J/G's list and the family dog.

"Another thing," she said. "I want to know exactly how that tape got on the air. That was *your* fault, Jack."

Damn, she was good. She and I both knew what had happened, but he didn't, and the doubt could work to our benefit. I was so proud of her that I could have died, had I not been dying already.

"We don't know yet," he said irritably. "We're working on it."

"How hard?"

Vanessa laughed, startling all of us. Cassie glared at her and then noticed my presence for the first time. She smacked the paper into Jack's chest and made straight for the couch. As hard as I tried, I couldn't figure out which one of her to watch; there appeared to be two all of a sudden.

"Hi," I said to the one on the right.

"Over here, Devvy," the other one said. "What's the matter with you? You look terrible."

"Oh, I don't know," Vanessa remarked. "I think she's kind of cute."

The Cassie on the left gave her the worst look I'd seen in a while. "Nobody asked *you.*"

"What's going on over there, Harper?" Jenner asked.

"Quiet, sir," Jack snapped, "or we'll miss something."

Cassie ignored that. She put a cool hand on my forehead. "What have you been doing?"

"Caffeine poisoning," I said. "Here."

Suspicious, she took the mug, sniffed it and then took a sip. "Espresso. How much?"

"All of it."

"I saw her," Vanessa said helpfully. "She chugged it. Maybe it was hot. That would hurt."

"If you were actually good for anything," Cassie said, "you would go find her some Advil or something. But I don't suppose —"

"Is somebody sick?" Jenner asked Jack.

"With any luck, sir," he said, "all three of them are. Maybe we'll get to watch."

Dying or not, I wasn't going to stand for that sort of thing. I shook Cassie off and wobbled up onto my feet. "The minute I feel better, Jack, your head comes off."

"Which one?" he asked in his best choirboy tone.

"Stop it," Cassie said, steadying me. "Vanessa? Advil? *Now?*"

Vanessa got up, smoothing her skirt. "Oh, all right. Do you want some ice, too?"

"Ice would be good," Cassie replied. "Right away would be even better."

For a second, I thought Vanessa was going to talk back. But then she shrugged, smiled and gave Cassie a pointed once-over. "I'll be right back, then."

Both Vanessas sashayed across the carpet and to the door. Both Jenners and Jacks watched every step. Both Cassies saw that I was watching, too, and sat me down on the couch, none too gently.

"If it's not proprietary information, Mr. Jenner," she said, "I'd love to know what that she-beast is doing here."

"*Is* she a beast, sir?" Jack asked, interested.

As best I could tell, Jenner winked at him.

"Never mind," Cassie said. "Devvy isn't feeling well. Why don't we just get this meeting over with, and then —"

"Meeting. Yes. We were meeting." Jenner gave his lapels a businesslike tug. "We were talking about that press conference. We were deciding what to do about it. Isn't that right, Harper?"

"As rain, sir."

Cassie snorted, but only loud enough for me to hear. She perched on the arm of the couch and started massaging the back of my neck with one hand. Grateful, I closed my eyes, leaning back into her touch.

"Derry?" Jenner asked.

"Sir?"

"Are you ill?"

I pried my eyes open. "A little."

"Can you think?"

"More or less."

"Good," he said. "I pay you for that. Think about what we can do."

"All right." I thought. It hurt. "Mr. Jenner?"

"Derry?"

"You were saying something about lawyers when I came in. Are we having lawyer trouble over this?"

"Tell her, Harper," Jenner instructed.

"You won't mind if I listen," Cassie said coolly. "Of course, I wouldn't have any ideas of my *own*, but—"

"Of course not, Miss Wolfe."

Cassie's grip tightened, making me wince. "Excuse me?"

Hazily, I saw Jack lean over to whisper to him. "I mean, of course I don't mind if you listen, Miss Wolfe. Go on, Mr. Harper."

"God, I love this job," Jack said. He might have elaborated, but one look from Cassie got him right down to business.

Closing my eyes again as she resumed her massage, I tried to follow whatever logic there was in what he was saying. Apparently, there'd been all kinds of lawyer trouble. The station managers were upset; the traffic managers were upset; the clients whose ads were supposed to run in those slots were beyond upset. I guessed we were talking several thousand dollars' worth of make-goods, not to mention a lot of impossible explanations to other agencies. The only party not injured by the situation was Rumours; the owners had called Jenner overnight to thank him for the publicity.

And then there was the Family Foundation. Jenner had heard from that crowd overnight, too. It seemed that J/J/G was going to get all the free publicity it could handle. According to a friend of a friend of a friend of Jenner's who had connections inside the foundation, Howard Abner was already working on a new speech for tomorrow's press conference. The friend of the friend of the friend heard that Abner had asked for research material, including Indigo Girls CD's and tapes of "Ellen."

"Christ, it was two seconds, tops," I complained. "You can hardly see anything. Besides, the last segment goes a lot farther, and that's obviously a girl and a boy."

Jack smiled big. "People can see a girl and a boy any time, Kerry. They can see that at the mall, even. But a girl and a girl ... well, people would pay money for that."

"People who live under a rock," Cassie said scornfully as the door opened. "And speaking of—"

"Welcome back," Jenner said to Vanessa. "Here — let me help you with that."

She favored him with a little smile as he relieved her of her terrible burden: a packet of Advil and an ice bag.

"Who are these for?" he asked.

"Devvy," Vanessa said.

Cassie bristled. " Devlin to you."

"Who are they talking about, Harper?" Jenner asked.

"Derry, sir," Jack said happily. "Have I mentioned lately how much I love this job?"

Vanessa resumed her place on the couch, while Cassie took the ice and Advil from Jenner. "Here," she said to me. "Take these. No, not with *that.*" She took the mug away and handed it to Vanessa. "You forgot water."

"I'm not a gofer," the woman said.

"Not a very good one," Cassie agreed.

"Miss Vanessa?" Jenner said. "They want water. As a favor to me?"

Vanessa sighed, got back up, and made a show of smoothing her skirt again before she left to find water.

"She needs a last name in the worst way," Cassie remarked to Jenner, pressing the ice bag against my neck. It was startlingly cold, making me jump. "Hold still, Devvy. ... Does she have a job description, Mr. Jenner?"

Jenner settled on the couch. "Special assistant."

"I see. Exactly how special?"

He frowned slightly, not sure he'd heard right. "Excuse me, Miss Wolfe?"

"You've got Rita Sanchez for an admin. She's the best in town. What else can you possibly need an assistant for?"

"This is so great," Jack said to himself, leaning comfortably against the wall.

Jenner glanced at him uncertainly. "Special projects?"

"I see." Cassie shifted the position of the ice bag slightly. "Well, this situation sounds like a *very* special project. Maybe we should give Vanessa a chance to demonstrate her many talents."

If we'd been alone, I would have kissed her. Damnation, the woman was good.

"Interesting," Jenner mused. "I think you have something there, Miss Wolfe. I think Miss Vanessa might just be uniquely qualified for this one."

"I thought she would be," Cassie said. "Oh, look; there she is again."

We all turned to watch her come back. She took the attention as her due and handed me a small paper cup without comment. Then she simply stared at Jenner.

"Chivalry, sir," Jack prompted.

Just that once, Jenner understood something; he shot up off the couch and offered her the vacant space.

"Thank you, Mr. Jenner," Vanessa cooed. "Such a thoughtful gentleman."

Cassie almost lost control of the ice bag, which nearly went down my shirt. "Sorry." With her free hand, she handed me the Advil. "Down the hatch with those. Right now."

I was starting to feel a little better but knew that tone and took the caps anyway. Everyone watched, as though they'd never seen anything like it before.

"Stop that," I said.

Vanessa smirked, letting her eyes travel.

"Especially you," I added.

She laughed out loud. "I don't think they like me very much, Mr. Jenner."

"They don't like anyone very much," he assured her. "Now, where were we, Harper?"

"Special projects," he said.

"That's right. Thank you, Harper. You know the situation, Miss Vanessa."

"I do."

"We've decided to give you a chance to handle it."

Her eyes lit up. "Really?"

"Really," Jenner said. "We'll give you an office and an admin. Whatever you need. Just come up with something brilliant."

"That doesn't cost a lot," Jack added.

He nodded. "That doesn't cost a lot, and that we can have by the end of the day."

"I'll get right on it, Mr. Jenner," Vanessa said. "Thank you so much for the opportunity."

Cassie cleared her throat significantly. "Well, if that's all, why don't we leave this in Vanessa's capable hands?"

"My pleasure," Jenner said. "That'll be all. Harper, Miss Vanessa, stay after."

"Thank God," Cassie muttered, getting up off the armrest. "Come on, Devvy. Hold the ice bag there for me, and I'll help you down to your office."

"I'm not a child," I told her, starting to resent the coddling a little.

"Of course not. You're a responsible grownup who just drank five or six cups of espresso all at once, just to see what would happen. I'm sure it was all in the interest of science. Give me your arm."

"I thought you said they were lovers, Jack," Vanessa said.

He laughed. "You'll get used to it. ... Have a nice day, ladies."

"Have a massive coronary," Cassie said sweetly and led me away.

∞ ∞ ∞

Cassie called her doctor from my office, to tell him what had happened and to find out whether I was going to live. Reassured that I would, she left for her next appointment, but not before she told Heather to keep me away from coffee for the rest of the day. Or so Heather reported when she came in to check on me.

"By the way, Troy and I tried to call you all night last night," she said. "What happened? How in the world did that tape get on TV?"

"I have no idea," I lied. "But I don't want to talk about it. Jenner's letting Vanessa handle it."

"Oh, Lord. That's trouble."

"I don't doubt it. Where's Kurt?"

"At the Hairport shoot. He was up half the night trying to call you, too." She smiled. "You'll like this, Dev — he said to tell you that he didn't do it."

"I'm not accusing him." A thought occurred to me. "Yet. What do *you* think?"

Heather looked over her shoulder to make sure the door was shut. Then she leaned forward confidentially. "I think he might lose his job if he did it. I'm not trying to suggest anything, though."

"No. And I didn't hear anything." We exchanged conspiratorial smiles. "Well, if he's out of the office today, we should be able to get some work done. How are you coming along with —" The local line buzzed. "Hold on a second. ... Kerry."

Sanchez said a few words and then hung up. I listened to the dial tone for a second before doing the same.

"Something wrong, Dev?"

"We'll find out. Vanessa just handled the Family Foundation thing."

"Trouble," Heather said darkly.

∞ ∞ ∞

It was really very simple, Vanessa said. If another model tries to embarrass you by telling stories behind your back, you tell worse stories to her face.

"I don't understand," Jenner said plaintively.

It was like this, Vanessa explained. If she says you have implants, you tell her she does, too, and they're pointing in different directions. If she says you had your butt done —

"I still don't understand. Besides, I don't think Howard Abner has implants. Does he, Harper?"

Jack glowered at him. "I wouldn't know, sir."

Here was the deal, Vanessa said, losing patience. We would send people to the press conference, and if Abner's people said embarrassing things about us, our people would say even more embarrassing things back, like who died and made them God, and when was the last time they got laid, and —

"I see. Yes, I see now. I like it," Jenner said.

Vanessa wasn't quite finished. Models were vicious, she said, so you could never rest easy; you always had to be planning your next attack. We'd have to do the same.

"Of course," Jenner said, nodding sagely. "We can't let the scheming bastards sneak up on us. What will we do?"

She was still working out the details, she said, but she thought it would be fun to do an ad campaign for ourselves.

Jenner's face clouded again. "I don't understand."

Vanessa consulted the little notepad she'd brought with her. Not for ourselves exactly, she said, but for (her lips moved silently, testing the word before she tried it) diversity. We could do a few public-service announcements, maybe.

"PSA's?" Jack asked, disbelieving. "At our rates?"

Well, she said, too casually, if he didn't believe in the First Amendment ...

For the first time all meeting, I raised my head out of my hands. Either there was still too much caffeine in my blood, or the woman was a lot sharper than she let on. Maybe the squirrel that ran the wheel that turned the gears in her brain was working overtime.

"Never mind what Harper believes, Miss Vanessa," Jenner said quickly. "Go on. What kind of campaign?"

"I'll leave the details to the experts," she said, looking at me. Proactively, I scowled back.

Jack noticed and laughed. "That would be Kerry, all right. Why don't we let her and Wolfe handle it, sir? They're pretty diverse."

I resented that some. "Now, just a goddamn min —"

"I've got it," he continued, fighting to keep a straight face. "We'll do a whole series. We'll call it 'Rainbows for Peace.' What do you think, Dev?"

I didn't have to think — I hated it — but Jenner seized on it as though it were Microsoft stock. "Outstanding, Harper. Derry, you're on it as of today. Miss Vanessa, excellent work. Outstanding. You have all of our resources at your disposal."

"As long as they don't cost much," Jack cautioned.

"Money be damned," Jenner said. "What do you think you'll need, Miss Vanessa?"

She turned on that feline smile. "I already have what I'll need, Mr. Jenner. But could I make a suggestion?"

"Of course. Please do."

"I think Devlin and Cassandra should be the ones to go to the press conference."

For a moment, I was glad Cassie wasn't there; she would've made a scene. "Not a chance," I said.

"I think Miss Vanessa's got a point, sir," Jack said. "They're both pretty disruptive."

Jenner nodded — perhaps in agreement, perhaps because his meds were wearing off; it was hard to tell these days.

"Sir, we can't do that," I protested. "Someone might recognize us from TV."

"Oh, don't worry about that," Vanessa said. "We'll have you two go in disguise. Just like Halloween."

Jack almost cracked a rib laughing.

"Not *just* like Halloween, Derry," Jenner said, very seriously. "And take a couple of normal people with you."

I excused myself then, just barely containing the urge to throttle Vanessa's squirrel on the way out.

Chapter Ten

Wednesday

"This is the stupidest thing I've ever done," Cassie whispered.

It was fairly high up on my list, too, but this wasn't the time or place to discuss it. Shoving blonde hair out of my eyes again, I gave her a warning look. The wig didn't fit right, and one long strand in front wanted to hang straight down, which might have passed in a bad-hair rock band but not at a Family Foundation press conference. The costume didn't fit very well, either. I'd borrowed it from Heather, who'd borrowed it from her mother, who apparently hadn't heard that shoulder pads were out. Uncomfortable, I tried to shift the drape of the jacket, but the cut was just too narrow for comfort. I was trapped in a pink-wool straitjacket for the duration.

Worse, Cassie had pinned her Egyptian junior stewardess brooch on the lapel. I wondered whether I could accidentally on purpose lose it. The clasp might be loose, after all, and if it wasn't, I could certainly make that happen. Furtively, I reached for it ...

... and got spiked by a stiletto heel. "Ow!"

"Don't even think about it, Devvy. If I have to look stupid, *you* have to look stupid."

I regarded her critically. "Stupid" was one word for it, all right. Her coloring was all wrong for the brunette wig, and the long ringlets didn't work, but none of that was as bad as the makeup. I'd never seen lipstick quite that color, even under fluorescent light. Neither did I like the giant hoop earrings or the bandanna tied around her head. True, she'd had the good taste to wear my black DKNY jacket, but otherwise, she looked like an explosion in Stevie Nicks' closet. In fact, I thought I'd seen that gypsy skirt onstage.

"What?" she asked.

"The whole point was to blend in, Cass."

"The whole *point* was to be in disguise. I'd say we are. Nobody recognizes us."

Well, she had me there. It had taken Heather and Troy a minute to identify us and then several more minutes to stop laughing. Troy had wanted to know whether my pink silk shirt was really polyester and had gotten his hand smacked by Cassie for trying to find out. (I had one of my own shirts on under that shirt, so it wouldn't have mattered, but she said that wasn't the point.) Thank God the suit skirt hadn't fit; if it had,

I'd have had to find pink shoes, too. Cassie didn't think the shoes I had on instead went with the jacket, but I wasn't taking any fashion advice from *her* today.

With a heavy sigh, I checked the time again. The press conference had been supposed to start at 10:00. They had a full house for this thing, including local TV crews, and you would think that someone would know not to keep vultures waiting.

I was starting to suggest that we leave and just let Heather and Troy deal with it when several men in blue suits filed across the stage. As they sat down in the row of folding chairs, I did a quick inventory. All of them had on white shirts and red ties, and unless I missed my guess, those little pins in their lapels would be flags. We might as well be at a Rotary meeting or maybe the Elks Club. Involuntarily, I smiled. My father sometimes did the antler thing for us kids when he was in a silly mood, and if I stood up and did it right now, probably every male in the room would return it. After they stoned me, of course, because only men were allowed to be Elks in this town.

"I think I went out with the one on the end," Cassie mused.

That remark sobered me right up. Narrowly, I examined the suspect. "You've got to be kidding."

"The third one from the left looks familiar, too. I'll go talk to him after, just to —"

"No talking to anyone," I said grimly. "You'd blow our cover."

She laughed and leaned against my shoulder. "I believe you're jealous."

"Not so damn loud. And get off me in public."

"Touchy," she remarked, giving me a little tickle.

I dropped my shoulder and pushed, shoving her off just in time; Howard Abner had just appeared at the podium.

There wasn't much exceptional about Abner except that he was about the size of a small steer. He'd played football at some Southern college — Alabama, maybe, or Texas — and still looked like it. If I remembered right, he'd been a center. I wondered whether he'd played many games without a helmet and whether that was his problem.

He hunched over the microphone. "Good morning, ladies and gentlemen. How are you all today?"

"We're fine, Mr. Rogers," Cassie whispered poisonously. "We had sex last night. Can you say that? I *knew* that you —"

"Quiet," I growled.

"... see you all here this morning," Abner was saying. "I'm sorry it's not a very pleasant occasion, but we'll talk about that and see what we can come up with to make things better. I'd like to start by showing you a little film we just made. But before I do, are there any children in the room?"

As if on cue, a baby wailed. Every head in the room turned. The woman who'd brought the creature patted its back worriedly, trying to soothe it.

"I don't think this is suitable viewing material for a young child, ma'am," Abner said.

There were a few snorts of laughter from the section where most of the reporters were sitting; I would have laughed, too, if Cassie hadn't elbowed me. Dutifully, the mother got up and left the auditorium. Abner watched her go, and only when the doors closed behind her did he push a button on the podium. A large projection screen slid down from a slot in the ceiling at the back of the stage.

"Lights, please, Jimmy," Abner said, "and roll it when you're ready."

Cassie leaned close as the lights went out. "I hope it's *9-1/2 Weeks.*"

This time, I elbowed her. Then I turned my full attention to the screen, where the Family Foundation logo was just bleeding in to the sound of herald trumpets. A few frames later, the title, "A Moral Crisis in Our Living Rooms," appeared over the logo, and drums thundered on the soundtrack, echoed by a patter of applause in the auditorium. I guessed that we were in for a bumpy morning.

Next, Abner himself appeared on the screen. The footage might have been shot in his office or on some foundation flunky's idea of a set; at any rate, it was heavy on eagles and American flags. He was holding a script that he would never look at, gazing sincerely into the camera, looking for all the world like a politician except for the big gaudy ring on his right hand. Maybe it was a football award or some ill-advised gift from the Little Lady.

I smiled at Heather, who was having a hard time not laughing out loud. When I talked to Jack about raises at the end of the year, I'd have to talk to him about promoting her, too. Kurt wouldn't like it, but I'd just piece him off with a meaningless title that sounded like a promotion. Head writer for special projects, say. And if he gave me enough trouble about it, I could see to it that those projects were *really* special.

Maybe I'd team him up with Vanessa, come to think of it. That would solve two problems at once and also amuse me no end. If I worked it just right —

"You're thinking," Cassie whispered. "Stop it."

I sighed, focusing on the film again. Abner had apparently wrapped up his opening remarks, because now we were seeing a series of clips — still photos of print ads and excerpts from TV spots, accompanied by snippets of radio commercials. I recognized some of my own work, some of Kurt's and a few pieces by rival agencies: Ad House, MediaComm, Llewellyn & Bates. None of it struck me as being particularly immoral except for the gallons of lip gloss on the Hardware City girl. Of course, we'd used glycerin on the models in the Club West ads, but they'd all refused to actually sweat, and besides, that was different.

The last clip went to black, and we were back in Abner's office.

"What do all these examples share in common?" he asked. "They all ..."

"Redundant," I whispered to Cassie.

"I told you to stop thinking," she whispered back.

"... to the climate of degeneracy that surrounds us," Abner said on-screen. "By repeated exposure, they weaken our resolve to lead moral lives. But worst of all, they give our children ideas that children should simply not have. I give you an example that speaks for itself."

Cassie braced herself, sensing what was coming. For my part, I was already resigned and just rode it out while the Rumours commercial played. Somewhere in the back, a woman made indignant noises.

I counted down the seconds in the first segment and waited. It wasn't likely that Abner had gotten hold of the version from Monday night, but ...

"Oh, hell," Cassie said.

... somehow, he had, and there Cassie and I were on the big screen.

"My dear Lord," someone wailed over a rising tide of horrified murmurs.

I thought we should leave and was about to suggest it when Heather ruined everything. Troy was trying to chase her down, but she was smaller, quicker and mad as a hornet, and before he caught up with her, she was on the stage, pushing buttons all over the podium. It took a few tries, and the house lights went off and on a couple of times, but she finally got the screen going back up into the ceiling before Abner could stop her.

"Whatever happens," Cassie whispered fiercely, "we do *not* know her."

I was all for that. Putting a serious look on my face, I tried very hard to look like somebody else.

Abner finally seized control of the podium, but only after Troy pulled Heather away. "What do you think you're doing, young lady?" Abner shouted.

"What do you think *you're* doing?" she shot back. "Where did you get this tape?"

"It was on Channel 5 Monday night. Every schoolchild in this city might have seen it, so don't —"

"That was an *accident*, you jerk. That was for our Christmas-party reel."

Abner frowned. "What reel? Where are you from, little lady?"

"Heather ..." Troy warned.

She ignored him. "J/J/G Advertising. And those are our *friends* you're trying to smear."

The audience began to murmur again. "If you love me, you'll kill her," Cassie demanded.

I did and would have, but in the very next heartbeat, things got even worse. A dark-haired woman in black stood up a few rows in front of us and waited for quiet. She got it, along with total attention. I had a very bad feeling about her. From the back, she looked a lot like —

"Ma'am?" Abner said, tentatively. "Did you have something to say?"

"Only that the young lady has very peculiar taste in friends," Monica said.

Well, no wonder she'd looked like Monica. Cassie muttered a string of curses — softly and without any particular emphasis, but with unmistakable venom.

"Thank you, ma'am," Abner said. "I think we all agree that —"

"I haven't quite finished, Mr. Abner. I also want to say that I'm shocked by that display. Such deviant behavior. God made Adam and Eve, not Madam and —"

"Hey!" Heather interrupted. "I know you. You were Dev's date at the Halloween party!"

Shocked, Cassie stopped her mantra in the middle of a word.

"Young lady," Abner said, "I hardly think this is the time or place for social —"

"Shut up and learn something," Heather said. "Dev's a *girl*."

Monica laughed. "I didn't say she wasn't. I just said she was deviant." Then she turned and pointedly looked at me. "Hello, Devlin. Interesting look. Something to hide?"

That did it. If I was about to go down in flames, I was at least going to fly my own colors. As coolly as possible, ignoring the stares — including Cassie's — I stood, pulled off the wig and ripped off the pink monstrosities. "Jacket," I said to Cassie.

Without a word, she took it off and handed it over. She had a strange expression on her face, and an even stranger little smile, but there wasn't time to ask about it. "Out," I said.

She made room for me to pass, and I started up the aisle, putting the jacket on along the way. Dimly, I was aware of flashbulbs and the whir of tape in the press section — and Monica's laughter, and the whispers of shocked recognition — but I ignored all that, lasering in on the big man at the podium.

"Hey, Dev," Heather said brightly. "You look mad. What are you —"

“Sit,” I said, still focused on Abner. Troy pulled her off the stage, and I pushed Abner off the podium. He might have been able to stop me, but maybe not; Heather was right; I was mad.

“Equal time,” I growled at him and then leaned over the microphone. “Let’s make this simple, all right? I’ll put it in terms you people can understand. My name is Devlin Kerry, and I’m a deviant.”

“How do you spell that?” someone shouted from the press section.

“D-e-v-i-a-n-t. Now shut the hell up and let me finish.”

Abner bristled. “I won’t have that kind of language. And I don’t want your kind on my property.”

“Mutual,” I said, “but the question is what kind *is* my kind. Am I a deviant? Or just a degenerate? And what kind are *you?*”

“Call security,” Abner said to one of the men on the platform.

“Oh, no,” the man replied. “I might miss something.”

The audience started laughing — at Abner’s expense. Angrily, he reached into his jacket for a cell phone.

“You might miss something, too,” I said. “But if you want to call somebody, call your lawyers. J/J/G’s already got you for theft of property, libel, violation of copyright ... should I go on?”

Abner stopped pushing numbers and just stared at me. Then he let his phone hand drop.

“I haven’t even mentioned the other agencies. They have lawyers, too. At the end of the day —”

“At the end of the day,” he said angrily, “I’m still right with God, and you’re still damned.”

“Coming from *your* God, Mr. Abner, I’ll take that as a compliment.”

There was a brief spell of absolute silence. “Blasphemer,” Abner finally managed.

“Hypocrite,” I replied. “I haven’t mentioned this football that you’re so proud of, either. You were a center, weren’t you? Guy who bends over for the quarterback? Now, why would a big, God-fearing, straight guy let another guy touch him *there* for a whole afternoon?”

The phone dropped out of Abner’s hand and shattered on the floor. It was the only sound in the entire auditorium.

“Not counting night games and scrimmages, of course. That’s a whole lot of football. Whole lot of football players, too.”

Abner’s jaw worked, but he didn’t say a word.

“Do you know why football players pat each other on the butt?” I asked the audience conversationally. “Because it takes too long to take their helmets off and kiss.”

About half the room liked that; the other half was mostly drowned out by the whooping and whistling. I glanced back at the men on the stage; every single one of them was gaping at Abner.

"Now, that's going too far," Abner complained. "Football is a *manly* sport, and I don't appreciate your slanderous —"

"Likewise, Mr. Abner. I don't appreciate slander either. I also don't appreciate witch hunts, bed checks and cheap publicity stunts."

"Cheap, my ass! That video alone cost ..." An instant too late, he realized what he'd said. Now all the laughter in the audience was hostile. He glared at everyone in general and then rounded on me. "I'll have you in court, you pervert. This is war."

"If you want a war, Jethro, you've got one. Have a manly day."

∞ ∞ ∞

Cassie was waiting for me in the parking lot, perched on the hood of her BMW. She'd taken off the wig, which was a vast improvement. I couldn't read her expression but started apologizing before I got there, to save time.

"Never mind," she said. "Come here."

Uncertain whether it was a good idea, I walked the rest of the way up to her — and barely caught her as she launched herself off the hood into my arms.

"You don't want to kill me?" I asked, bewildered.

"Eventually," she said and kissed me again. I finally had to push her off just to breathe.

"What was *that* for?"

"That little performance back there. It was kind of sexy."

"Are you feeling all right?" I asked.

She ignored the question. "When you took all that pink stuff off, it was kind of like Superman coming out of the phone booth."

"Superwoman. And 'out' would be the operative word," I muttered.

"That part's done. Come here again."

"We're at the Family Foundation," I reminded her.

"And they could use some sex education," she said, closing in.

Oh, to hell with it. I gave up and got into the spirit of the thing. But before I got all the way in, someone interrupted.

"Very clever," Monica said.

We broke off, and I pushed Cassie back toward the car, where she might be safer. "You sound surprised," I said to Monica.

"But very foolish. Don't think this is done."

"If *you* want a war, too, Monica, I'll pencil you in."

For a second she might have smiled. Then she disappeared — this time in an impressive pillar of flame.

"She is so Old Testament sometimes," I said to Cassie. "Forget her. How about lunch?"

Cassie smiled. "I've got a better idea."

As it turned out, she did. We didn't quite make it back to the office until mid-afternoon.

Chapter Eleven

Later Wednesday

Cassie let me off a couple of blocks from the agency; she wanted to stop by a client's office to drop off a contract, and the fastest way was the street we were already on. That was fine. I promised to be at her house at 7:00, with whatever wine went with the spinach-walnut pesto from the gourmet pasta place; she promised to get basil pasta, too, if I would pick up some Ben & Jerry's. After dinner, she might put on a few jazz CD's and start the whirlpool, and if I was really good, she'd use the Porthault sheets.

"Do you ever listen to us when we talk like this?" I asked her, curious.

"Of course not, honey. Now kiss me goodbye."

Bemused, I leaned back into the Beemer. All right, we were yuppie scum, both of us, depraved beyond shame. Decent People didn't talk this way, and they didn't go to such bother about things. They'd have macaroni and cheese out of the blue boxes and plain vanilla ice cream, and if they decided to take a bath later, they would damn sure not take a radio in the bathroom with them. Cassie and I knew all that. We'd both been brought up along the straight and narrow. Where had we gone wrong?

And what the devil had taken us so long to go?

When Cassie finally felt sufficiently kissed, she took off in a screech of burning rubber — showing off, I guessed, or having fun just because she could. As much as her driving worried me sometimes, I couldn't help smiling; she thought that car of hers was a toy, and I imagined a ten-year-old Cassie pedaling furiously in rush-hour traffic, daring anyone to catch her, pink streamers flying from the handlebars ...

Startled, I blinked hard. What had gotten into me? There I was, standing on a busy street corner thinking about macaroni and cheese, bathtub safety and pink Schwinns, when in fact, I'd just spent two hours horizontal in the middle of a work day, doing things that I certainly hadn't been brought up to do. A fine time to have a family-values flashback.

Then again, I'd just spent the morning among Decent People; maybe they were contagious. Shaking the image off, I turned and started walking fast toward J/J/G.

∞ ∞ ∞

My first clue should've been the TV trucks parked along 10th. That wasn't unusual, though. We were downtown, not far from the media strip, and real city-dwellers are immune to unusual anyway; it had been years since I'd consciously heard a siren.

The second clue didn't wait for me to catch it. Chip was pacing on the sidewalk in front of the lobby door, and the instant we saw each other, he practically sprang at me.

"Not this way," he said. "Around the back."

"Why? Is there a client in the lobby?"

"Where's Cassie?"

"Dropping a contract. Why?"

He pushed me toward the sidewalk that led to the back of the building. "Not here. C'mon."

"Chip, son, I've already had a long day. If you want to play Mulder and Scully, find someone your own —"

"Reporters," Chip said flatly.

"Reporters?"

"In the building."

"Why?"

He gave me a look that he had to have learned from Cassie.

"You're not serious," I said.

"I'm very serious. Channel 12's in Jenner's office right now. Come on, before somebody sees you."

"It's a little late, Chip. Thanks, but —"

"Kurt's up there, too."

My professional life flashed before my eyes, and the writing on the wall went by like a news ticker: ...REPORTERS...JENNER...KURT...

Trouble.

"Stay here and watch for Cassie," I said to Chip. "Don't let her in the building."

"She won't like that."

"No. But *I* won't like it if reporters get hold of her. Which one of us do you want mad at you?"

Cassie would throw a fit if she found out that he didn't have to think about the answer. "I'll take care of her. Be careful, Dev."

"Too late," I said and made straight for the front door.

∞ ∞ ∞

It has always been my experience that when you have murder on your mind, people get out of your way. True, the long black raincoat might have helped, or the speed at which I was moving, but people practically dived behind things all over the lobby as I passed through. One fool didn't react fast enough, so I went right through him, not even breaking stride. It felt surprisingly good.

To keep the black adrenaline running, I took the stairs. A girl from Research was heading down at the same time; wisely, she flattened herself against the stairwell wall to let me pass, losing all her papers in the process. At any other time, I'd have apologized; this time, *she* did.

Finally, I reached Jenner's outer office. Sanchez was bravely trying to ward off a pack of media types with the business end of her phone, which was ringing. Pushing through the crowd, I took the phone and hung up for her.

"You look like you could use a break, Rita," I said evenly. "Why don't you let me take over for a while?"

She puzzled over the offer for a second; then she got it, and she smiled. "Thanks, Dev. I owe you."

"Don't mention it. Go on now."

Uncertain what to do, the reporters stood there slack-jawed, watching her go. I took advantage of their distraction to put all the lines except one on hold. Then I dialed.

"There's a disturbance at J/J/G Advertising," I said softly when the dispatcher answered. "On the fourth floor. Can you send a car?"

"What kind of disturbance, ma'am?"

"Press. Some of them are ugly. You might want to send the SWAT team."

There was a pause. "Is anyone in danger, ma'am?"

"Everyone," I promised and hung up.

Only then did the reporters catch on. "Jesus!" someone shouted. "That's the one from the press conference!"

I was already halfway to Jenner's office and didn't even turn. A cameraman tried to jump in my path, but I fixed his wagon with one well-aimed knee. Then, pushing the body aside, I threw Jenner's door open and slammed it shut ... on a reporter part. The reporter to whom it belonged howled in pain; I waited two seconds, kicked the foot back into the outer office and slammed the door shut again, taking care to lock it.

Then I surveyed the scene with a cold eye. It was about what I'd expected — Jenner, Jack and Kurt for our side; a lacquered anorexic and a scruffy cameraman for theirs. Well, that should be easy enough to knock off.

"Thank God you're here, Derry," Jenner said. He looked a little wilted from that distance, as though he'd sweated through his shirt.

Maybe he had; TV lights were hot enough when you had a clear conscience.

I ignored him and lasered Kurt, who jumped like a guilty lizard and tried to hide behind Jack — who, ever valiant, was trying to hide behind Jenner. It was so Larry, Moe and Curly that if Jenner had half a wit, he'd have been trying to hide behind Kurt.

Whatever they'd told the press, I was definitely going to hate it.

"Keep rolling," the anorexic ordered the cameraman. Then, putting on a bright professional expression, she started walking toward me. "Devlin Kerry? I'm Lisa Hartwell from Eyewitness —"

"Camera off," I said to her.

She tried to look sympathetic. "I'm really sorry, but we're here on a news story. My assignment editor wants —"

"Camera off or no comment."

"But I've already interviewed all these people here — on camera. They've already told me —"

I tapped the crystal of my watch. "Ten seconds."

For nine seconds, she simply stared at me. On the stroke of the tenth, she turned and nodded to the cameraman, who set the camera back on his shoulder and made a show of pressing a button. What they didn't know was that I wasn't stupid. I'd made too many commercials not to know the parts of a camera by now, and what he'd pushed wasn't the power button.

What they *also* didn't know was that they'd just done exactly what I wanted.

"It's off, Ms. Kerry," the reporter lied. "Can I ask you a few questions now?"

"Of course," I said.

∞ ∞ ∞

A few minutes later, many, many police arrived, and in the confusion, I slipped out. It was a shame to miss all the fun, but my work there was done. Besides, Cassie would be back by now, and although I trusted Chip's good intentions, I doubted that they were a match for her temper.

Sure enough, she was sprinting up the hall — no small feat in those heels — as I was strolling down it. Chip was doing his best to keep up with her, but the frustration was plain on his face.

"Cops," I heard Cassie mutter. "We're too late. She killed them all."

I leaned back against the wall, smiling widely, and waited. When she reached me, she simply wrapped herself around me and held on.

"I won't let them take you, Devvy," she vowed. "I'll chain myself to you, if I have to, but —"

"Kinky," I said, "but you won't have to."

She pulled back, puzzled. "What?"

"They're here for the reporters. This floor is private office space, and they weren't invited, so I called 911."

"Oh, thank God," she said, collapsing back on my shoulder. "I really don't want to go to jail."

"I really don't think you should anyway. Those orange coveralls would look terrible on you." She didn't laugh, so I stroked her hair reassuringly and nodded at Chip, who was leaning against the opposite wall trying to catch his breath. "You tried. I understand."

"We should still get her out of here," he said.

"We should get *all* of us out of here. Where are Troy and Heather?"

"Out looking for you, last I heard. They ought to be back any time."

"Tell them what happened. Then all of you clear out. I'll get her home. Call us around —"

"I'm turning off the phones," Cassie said into my shirt.

I frowned slightly. Something was wrong; she wasn't the clingy type, but she wasn't letting go for love or money. "Call us after the 6:00 news," I told Chip. "Use my cell number. Then we'll figure out what to do next. All right?"

"All right, but ..." His expression grew even darker as he glanced over my shoulder. "Better get her out of here now, Dev."

"I'm all over it. ... C'mon, Cass. Time to leave. Want to let go now?"

"No."

I sighed. "Orange coveralls. Not a good look."

She said something I couldn't quite hear and then pushed away.

"Attagirl," I said. "We'll take the back stairs."

∞ ∞ ∞

We didn't go quite straight to her house; she insisted on stopping by the wine shop and the pasta place and Ben & Jerry's anyway. She also insisted on making a detour to my condo, for the purpose of packing a suitcase. If we were going to have to bunker down somewhere for a couple of days, she said, we were going to do it at *her* house.

So it was close to an hour later that we finally got around to comparing notes. I made her go first; she'd find out soon enough what I'd been up to.

Cassie had had a bad adventure herself, it seemed. She'd stopped by Sanders Travel with the contract, expecting to drop it and run, but the client had heard what happened at the Family Foundation and insisted on having a chat. Sanders Travel had wanted to jazz up its image, he'd said, but not quite *that* much, so he'd decided against working with us. Although he personally had an open mind — why, some of his best friends were gay — it wouldn't be good for business for him to get involved with J/J/G now. Oh, yes, he was sure that many of his customers were gay, or maybe just not actively antigay, but a lot more of them had families, and —

I started to jump all over the "families" part, but she was way into storytelling mode and just kept going. Sanders thought he'd pass on advertising right now, to let the publicity blow over — and in the meantime, why didn't she meet him for dinner at the Meridian Club one night soon? Better yet, why didn't she bring me along? He had the key to a private suite upstairs, and he'd be happy to do business with J/J/G later, if only the three of us —

"Car keys," I growled, not waiting for the rest.

"No, Devvy. It's all right. I told him ..." Barely in time, she grabbed the keys off the end table. "*No*."

"Don't make me hurt you."

She snorted and dropped the keys down the front of her blouse.

"Like that's going to stop me."

"Let me finish," she said. "I told him I know his wife — *and* his boyfriend. I *also* told him to close his mind before the rest of his brains fall out. Then I said —"

"I love you," I said with feeling. "Now give me the keys."

"Do you want to hear the rest of the story, or do you want to sleep on this couch tonight?"

Impatient, I gave her my fiercest Look. To my outrage, she started laughing.

"That won't work on me, Devvy. It's adorable, but it's no good."

"*Adorable?*"

"I saw this picture in a PBS catalog once. I think it was called 'Angry Bluebird,' and it looked exactly —"

"I do *not* look like a bluebird."

"Well, maybe not *just* exactly. You're taller. And darker. And a much better kisser, if I remember right." She leaned in to check her recollection, but I was having none of it. "Something wrong?"

"Not anymore," I said — and with one swift motion, fished out the keys. "Thanks. I'll be back."

"I'm not kidding about the couch," Cassie warned.

Torn between the need for a travel agent's blood and my even greater need for her, I wavered for a few seconds. Finally, I tossed the keys back on the end table, sulking.

"I'm not kidding about the bluebird, either," she added.

"Cassie ..."

She gave me a deceptively sweet smile and moved closer. "I told him that if you ever found out what he said, you'd do the same thing to him that you did to Howard Abner this morning — but only if you weren't in the mood to just rip his goodies off instead. That pretty much did it. We lost the contract, but he won't be any more trouble. Are you proud of me?"

"Yes. But don't do that again."

"I can't promise that."

"Try." As the anger started to drain off, I looked at her more closely. For all her big talk, then and just now, she still looked stressed. "So why were you so upset when I saw you right after? You just about strangled me."

"I got scared for a minute, I guess. It just hit me what kind of day we'd had. I saw you, and I saw all those police, and I thought ..." Sighing, she put her head on my shoulder. "I thought, 'I usually don't have this much trouble with relationships.' "

I laughed, pulling her closer. "Sorry."

"I'm not. But do me a favor — give me a little warning the next time you decide to go public? I think I'd like to sit the next one out."

"I don't think you can, Cass. Channel 12 —"

"Damn." She grabbed my wrist to check the time. "Almost 5:00. Can you reach the remote?"

I could, barely, and did. She sat up a little, frowning at the TV screen as she switched the set on and tuned it to Channel 12.

I really hoped she was in a forgiving mood.

Chapter Twelve

When the newscast broke for commercials, I finally worked up the nerve to look at Cassie. As expected, she was staring at me in mute horror and looked as though she'd been at it for a while.

"I had no choice," I said to her.

No response.

"She asked for it."

Still no response.

"You liked the attitude this morning," I said irritably. "You practically attacked me in the parking lot."

She didn't answer, but her eyes narrowed slightly in a way that I knew all too well. Small-craft warnings began to fly in my head.

"All right, it might have been a little much. But I had to do something. She asked me —"

"You kissed her," Cassie said abruptly.

Was that all? "Not really. I was trying to scare her."

"You were trying to scare her," she repeated.

Suddenly uncomfortable, I shifted on the couch. "Well, it worked. She ran like a rabbit. When the police —"

"I want to understand this," she said in a dangerously reasonable tone. "You were trying to scare her. By kissing her. Correct?"

"I didn't exactly."

"You didn't *exactly*. I see. And what did *she* do? Exactly?"

"You saw the tape. The part where it went crazy is where she ran over the cameraman. She just about jumped out —"

"That's not what I mean."

I knew it, but nothing good could come of that conversation. "There wasn't time to think, Cass. She was a problem. I solved it."

"Of course you solved it. You're associate creative director in charge of sex. What else would you do?"

"You're missing the point," I said, starting to get defensive. "I was trying to teach her a lesson. That camera was supposed to be off. She lied about it. So her cred goes right down —"

"Oh, there was a *point* in that. And you taught a lesson, too. You amaze me, pookie. I really ..."

"Don't call me pookie," I said between gritted teeth.

"... didn't expect you to try to convert the whole female population of the county on the 6:00 news, but ..."

"I wasn't *converting*. Would you just let me explain? I was —"

"...the witch let you off the leash, and now —"

"Stop now, while you can," I warned her.

"No. I'm nowhere *near* done."

"Cassie, don't make me mad."

"Don't make *you* mad? *I'm* not the one who goes around kissing every hussy who's had her shots."

Exasperated, I pushed her off, got up and got way out of her immediate vicinity. "She was going after *you* next, Cass. If you think I was going to let her get to you — if you think I'm going to let *anyone* get to you — you're insane. It was either kiss her or kill her, and I would've had a lot more fun the other way. What did you expect me to do? Just stand there and —"

"What do you mean, you would've had more fun the other way?"

I raised an eyebrow. She still looked furious, but her tone had just softened dramatically.

"Are you trying to tell me that you didn't enjoy it?" she asked.

"I'm not trying — I *am* telling you. And I didn't even *do* it. I would sooner have kissed an iguana. The woman —"

"Iguanas don't have lips," she said matter-of-factly.

"That's not the point. The point is ... the *point* is ..." I fumbled for something, anything, to fill in the blank and finally, in absolute frustration, kicked the nearest thing as hard as I could. Unfortunately, the nearest thing was the brick hearth. That was going to hurt. "Oh, hell, Cass, I don't *know* what the point is anymore. It seemed like a good idea at the time."

There was a very long silence across the living room. "An iguana, huh?" she finally asked.

Relieved, I smiled just a little. "Maybe a gecko. Something in the lizard family. I don't like any of them much."

"And, technically, you didn't kiss her?"

"Of *course* not."

"Devvy? Honey?"

Thank God that was over. "Sweetheart?"

"You didn't just break your foot, did you?"

"Not in these shoes. Maybe just a toe."

"Then you'd better get it in water right away. I'll go start the whirlpool."

"Will that help?"

"If you're lucky," she said.

∞ ∞ ∞

After about the dozenth ring, Cassie sent me to answer the door. She thought she was temporarily incapacitated, and besides, she still had about half a glass of wine left. If I hurried back, she said, she'd make it worth my while.

I didn't even bother to dry off — just threw on a robe on the way to the front door. It was only Chip, Troy and Heather, though. Damn, I'd forgotten about them. Heather was holding a videotape, most likely of the evening newscasts, so I would have to let them in for at least a second.

"You were supposed to call, weren't you?" I asked.

"We did call," Chip said. "We called your cell number, just like you said. Didn't you turn the phone on?"

Oh. What with one thing and another, I'd forgotten. "Never mind. Come in. But only for a minute."

They followed me into the foyer. Chip made a point of averting his eyes, which seemed strange until I remembered that I was standing there soaking wet in nothing but a robe.

"You probably already know this," Heather remarked, "but you're not dressed. Did we get you out of the tub?"

"Whirlpool."

Troy's face lit up. "Cassie's got a whirlpool? Where?"

"Master bath. It's just a little ... Hey!" I grabbed him just in time. "She's in it."

"Then what are you doing leaving her alone? People drown in bathtubs all the time!"

"Nice try, Troy."

He shrugged. "Can't blame me."

"No. But don't try it again." Brushing wet hair back out of my eyes, I turned to Heather. "So what's on the tape?"

She didn't answer right away; she was busy glaring at Troy, who was busy pretending not to notice. Interesting.

"Tape," I prompted.

Reluctantly, she broke off the ray on Troy and answered the question. "Newscasts. We thought you two would want to see them all, so we made a tape."

"We do. We'll run it later. Thanks. Now, if you don't mind ..."

"Dev?" she asked.

I was already halfway to the door, which I intended to deadbolt and chain behind them. "What?"

"Why are you limping?"

"It's nothing."

Not persuaded, she came over to see for herself. "I don't know about that. Your big toe's kind of purple. Does it hurt?"

Not much. Cassie had applied some highly creative therapy, so the toe not only didn't hurt too badly but was also in a very good mood. There was no reason to share that information, though. "It's all right. Just a bruise. Goodnight, Heather. We'll see you tomorrow."

Chip and Troy, taking the hint, headed out the door. Heather finally did, too, but then stuck her head back in.

"How did it happen? Did Cassie stomp you for kissing that reporter from Channel 12?"

"I didn't kiss her!"

"You didn't? It sure looked —"

"Don't believe everything you see," I snapped, and slammed the door.

∞ ∞ ∞

Somewhere in the dead of that night, something yanked me out of bed, and I hit the carpet like a rock.

"What the hell ...?"

"An apt choice of word," Monica said.

Grimacing, I raised my head off the floor a couple of inches. The hem of her black gown was practically in my face. I made a point of pushing it away, then grabbed a piece of the comforter and pulled myself up.

"Speaking of words, I want a few with you."

"That would make one of us," I said.

"Maybe I haven't made myself clear. This is not an option."

"It will be when Cassie wakes up," I said, louder than I'd intended. I glanced over, expecting the object of my affection to be awake, spitting flames, but she hadn't even stirred. That was more than just odd; I'd hit the floor so hard they'd probably heard the thump in China. "Cass?"

"She'll sleep through this. I want to talk to you in private."

I leaped back into the bed, pulse pounding as I checked Cassie's. It seemed regular and so did her breathing. "If you've done anything to her, I swear —"

"I would love to hear the end of that threat," Monica said, "but I have more important business with you. I want to know what you thought you were doing this afternoon."

"You'll have to be more specific. I had a pretty full afternoon. What did I think I was doing *when*?"

"When you kissed that blonde harlot from the TV station."

Of all the things I'd been expecting, that was the very last. "Blonde harlot?"

"You know very well what I'm talking about."

Suddenly, it occurred to me that I did. I'd been in trouble for the same thing all evening — first with Cassie, then with Heather, and now, apparently, with Monica. But why? Wasn't this just what she'd wanted?

"I'm waiting," Monica said ominously.

"You can wait till your hometown freezes. I don't owe you any explanation."

"You owe me *everything*. In case you've forgotten, you're not a free agent. Why did you kiss her?"

"*I didn't kiss her!*"

"Do you think I'm a fool?"

Unwisely, I was about to answer that question when it dawned on me: Monica didn't know that I'd stopped just short any more than Cassie had. Trouble was, Monica was *supposed* to know. After all, she was still my demon.

... Wasn't she?

"I could send you to the very worst part of hell," Monica warned.

"What? The Kathie Lee Gifford section?"

"Don't tempt me. I could do that."

"But then what would you do for an encore?"

Her eyes flared into red coals as she took a step back and raised one arm, index finger pointed straight at my heart. "This is your only warning, Devlin. I own you. You can't beat me by playing my game. If you ever try defying me again, I'll throw you to a pack of Alabama Baptists."

"You're slipping, Monica. You used to know everything about me. If you still *did*, you'd know the only threat you could make that would do any good —"

"I could send her with you," she snapped.

"She'd probably insist."

The fires in Monica's eyes abruptly went out, and for an instant, she looked uncertain. Then she shrugged, laughing it off. "Damning her would be redundant. She's already yoked to you for all eternity."

"Now, just one damn minute —"

"No more games," she growled — and disappeared without the pillar of fire. But this time, she left a whiff of sulfur behind.

I sat in the dark for a long time, thinking. Finally, I stretched out next to Cassie and bear-hugged her within an inch of her life. After a few seconds, she began to stir.

"Devvy?" She sounded half-asleep but otherwise totally normal. "Is something wrong?"

"Not with us," I said.

Chapter Thirteen

Thursday

The rain started again at dawn, and all the forecasts said we were in for a stretch of it this time. Typical weather for this time of year, though; we would see next to no sun from now until spring. Most people were already in a bad mood for the duration.

But not Cassie and certainly not me. True, we'd been up half the night, working. We'd rousted the troops — and Vanessa — out of bed for an early-morning meeting in my office, where Jenner would never think to look and Kurt would know not to try. We'd called in every IOU we had with the local TV stations to get air-check tapes of the newscasts. We'd even drafted a press release for Jenner. And of course we'd argued about every detail of what I wanted to do, down to the commas.

But then we'd taken my MG out to get pastry and good coffee for the meeting, and for the first time in living memory, she hadn't complained about how small the car was or how old my tape collection was or even about my taste in '80's music. I'd had a Blondie tape in the deck and ejected it, out of habit, but she'd put it back in. Then she'd directed me to pull into the park for just a minute. Somehow, we'd wound up parked under a tree for more than just a minute — long enough for the MG to get plastered with wet leaves, anyhow — and I was never going to hear "Call Me" the same way again.

I hoped this was just a phase, because I might not live through another two weeks of it.

"You two don't have to look so cheerful," Heather complained, rummaging through the pastry box. "It's raining again."

"And you're in big trouble," Troy added. "Well, *you* are, anyway, Dev."

Cassie shrugged. "She *is* trouble. Sue me — I like it."

Knowing the danger of saying anything in return, I let that one fly by without comment.

"You must," Heather said. "Hey, Dev, did I tell you my mother saw you on TV last night? She wanted to know if you're always like that. I said no — you're usually worse."

Laughter — friendly, but entirely at my expense. I assumed an injured expression and limped over to look out the window.

"Don't tease her," Cassie warned Heather. "She was in a good mood an hour ago. I'd like to keep it that way."

"What happened an hour ago?"

In the window glass, I saw Cassie beckon her close for confidential speech.

"No! In Bryant Park?"

"It's a little car," Cassie said to her as though that explained it.

Heather's reflection shook its head. "*Still.* Wow. I would never have thought Dev had it in her."

"Well," Cassie said, an evil note creeping into her voice, "it got out. And I can tell you exactly where it went."

I was seriously considering whether to jump out the window when the door opened and Vanessa walked in, putting an instant stop to the hilarity.

"Sorry I'm late. Did I miss anything?"

"No," I said, relieved. "We were just getting ready to run the newscasts. Coffee?"

She declined and started to move past me to the vacant chair. Then she rocked back on one heel, frowning slightly.

"Problem?" I asked her.

"Bite mark. At least it matches your sweater."

Instinctively, I reached up. Damn.

"Sorry, sweetie," Cassie said over the laughter.

"What would you call that color?" Heather asked the room at large. "The sweater, I mean. Maroon? Plum? Bruise?"

"If you want to see something in bruise," I growled, "keep talking."

Heather smirked. Mentally, I reduced her year-end raise by one percent.

"So much for that good mood," Troy said. "Maybe we ought to run those tapes now — I want to live through the day. Can we start with Dick Farmer?"

That worked for me. Cassie and I had always loved Dick Farmer — a mediocre reporter at best, but a man with a priceless name. We'd often speculated on what the schoolyard bullies had called him. Conveniently enough, the Channel 5 tape was at the top of the stack, so I pushed it into the machine.

"This is Dick Farmer," the man said soberly, "reporting from ..."

Troy, Heather and Chip lost it, honking and snorting with laughter; Cassie clearly wanted to, but refused to meet my eye. Sighing, I tossed the remote to Troy, who promptly rewound the tape.

As the tape — and the honking and snorting — started again, Vanessa reached up and pulled my sweater sleeve. I bent down obligingly. "Is that his real name?" she asked.

"Yes."

"Why doesn't he go by Richard?"

I considered. "Because it's not funny."

"Do *you* think it's funny?"

Uncomfortable, I straightened up. "Depends on my age at any given moment."

Vanessa didn't respond, but she gave me a look that I hoped Cassie didn't see. If I hadn't known better, I would've thought it was a come-on. Just to be safe, I decided to go stand by my beloved.

"What was all that about?" she asked.

"Dick Farmer."

She scowled at Vanessa and then made a point of leaning back against my shoulder. "That's enough, Troy. Play it through."

He obeyed, but only after he rewound the tape one more time. Then we watched the report in relative silence. Like Farmer, it was short, dull, humorless and missed the whole point. There'd been a press conference at the Family Foundation; an audience member had taken offense at a video; the foundation regretted the incident.

"Boring," Heather said. "Do Channel 10 next. That was kind of fun."

Too bad that we'd missed that one last night, then. Chip found the tape, and Cassie got a bit more comfortable.

Channel 10 was the Fox affiliate, so of course its version was kind of fun. The anchors introduced the story by saying that children should leave the Channel 10 viewing area. Then we got a taste of the foundation's video — the section with the actual ads — this time accompanied by "Bad to the Bone." After that, the report cut to my interruption of Howard Abner at the podium. Wincing, I wondered whether I looked that sinister in real life.

"Thank God she's on our side," Troy said, laughing.

I decided not to have heard that. Besides, the report had moved on to an interview with Abner, shot slightly from below so that he looked as large and self-satisfied as Mount Rushmore. "... and morality are not popular," he was saying, "but we're not in this to win any popularity contests. We're in it to fight for decency ..."

"And justice and the American way," Chip droned.

Heather shushed him. The reporter was back on now, saying something about reaction from ad agencies. A second later, Jenner's face was all over the screen. I relaxed slightly; he shot even more sinister than I did.

"We can't be responsible for our employees' private behavior," Jenner said.

"Is that an apology?" the reporter asked off-camera.

Jenner's eyes nearly crossed. Movement just behind him got my attention, and I suddenly realized what it was: Jack, holding him up physically and working him like Lamb Chop. By Jenner's expression, he was listening intently to something.

"No," he finally answered. "That employee is not responsible either. She was in a car accident a few months ago and hit her head."

Closing my eyes, I hit it again then, on purpose, on the wall, as the three slackers in the room burst into whistles and applause. Cassie made me stop, and she held her hand on the back of my head to keep me from doing it again.

"We'll be following this story for any future developments," the reporter promised. "Now back to you, Dave, in the studio."

Dave, in the studio, thanked him for his good work, and so did Jennifer, who was also in the studio but inexplicably not mentioned in the "back to," after which the station broke for a commercial — interestingly enough, one of mine.

"You've gotta love Fox," Chip said. "Now can we play the good one?"

No one had to ask which one he meant. Heather sailed the tape across the office to him; he made a nifty one-handed catch and stuck it in the machine.

"So Dev," Troy said, too casually, "is Lisa Hartwell a good kisser?"

Cassie gave me a very narrow look — she still wasn't entirely convinced — but reached back to lace her fingers with mine before she turned an even narrower look on him. "She didn't kiss her. You'll see."

"I *did* see. It looked to *me* like —"

"Play the tape, Troy," I ordered.

He did, leaning forward avidly as the story started. Vanessa, on the other hand, looked bored, but fashionably bored.

We watched in silence as the main story played out. All too soon, the camera was in Jenner's office, and he, Jack and Kurt were telling their versions of the truth, in which the agency was the victim of an employee with a recent head injury. Kurt helpfully added that I'd always had a temper anyway, and come to think of it, I'd tried to throttle him just a few weeks ago. Of course, he said, that might have had something to do with the fact that I hadn't actually had sex for many, many years, up until Halloween night, and if Ms. Hartwell wanted, he could arrange an interview with the woman who'd finally turned the trick, so to speak. Her name was —

That was when I'd broken in. Uncomfortable, I watched myself storm into the office, black raincoat, bad mood and all. As she had last night when she'd first seen that part, Cassie leaned back and whispered, "My hero."

"Heroine," I corrected. "And cut that out."

Unrepentant, she tightened her hold on my hand. As I had last night, I wondered what had gotten into her.

Heather cleared her throat elaborately. "If you two don't mind, we're trying to watch television here."

We both scowled at her but kept quiet for the interview.

> Her: Is it true, Ms. Kerry, that you threatened a holy war against the family?
>
> Me: No.
>
> Her: But it is true that you called Mr. Abner "Jethro" and promised him a war?
>
> Me: That was strictly personal.
>
> Her: But you *did* kiss a woman in that TV commercial, didn't you?
>
> Me: I can't wait to hear the point of that question.
>
> Her: Mr. Abner called you [consulting her notes] "a godless deviant."
>
> Me: Compared with what passes for normal in this town, "deviant" is a raise. Now, what does this have to do with anything? If you're asking about the Rumours ad, that scene was work footage. It got on the air by mistake.
>
> Her: Mr. Abner said you were trying to recruit young girls with it.
>
> [Brief silence]
>
> Me [moving slowly forward]: Kissing a woman on television could do that? Astonishing.
>
> Her: Mr. Abner also said ... I'm sorry, Ms. Kerry, you'll need to move back a little. The camera angle ...
>
> Me [still advancing]: You said the camera was off, Ms. Hartwell.
>
> Her: It was. I mean, it's supposed to be. I mean ...
>
> Me: Well, you'll be glad it's still on, Ms. Hartwell. This next part might jump-start your ratings.
>
> Her: What next part?

It was strange — I'd leaned down and over slightly so that the camera couldn't actually see, but in the split-second before it looked like I kissed her, it looked as though she'd moved to meet me. The tape cut away at the critical point, of course, but I wondered whether if we replayed it ...

There was no need to wonder, of course, because Troy was already rewinding. He ran it back several times, in slow motion and frame by frame. By the third time, Cassie was getting impatient.

"You're not going to see it, Troy, because it isn't there. It's just subtext."

"I don't care if it's spinach," he said to her. "I love it."

Cassie sighed. "I don't understand this. What *is* it with men? Women don't fantasize about seeing two of *you* together."

Privately, I didn't understand what was up with the Three Stooges, mud wrestling and "Baywatch," either. Well, all right, make that the Stooges and mud wrestling, but I still knew that there was no real excuse for "Baywatch."

"Boys will be boys. We can't help it."

"Do you even try?" Cassie shot back.

Troy looked genuinely surprised. "What for?"

Heather, Cassie and I lasered him. Vanessa still looked bored.

"Oh, c'mon," he protested. "I'm just kidding. Ask Chip."

"I wish you'd leave me out of these things from now on," Chip said wearily. "I took marketing in college, not anthropology. Can't we just see the rest of the tape before Kurt gets here?"

Another point for Chip. While Troy reluctantly started the tape again, I leaned slightly forward to have private words with Cassie. It was just a compliment on her flawless taste in protégés, but she gave me a little nuzzle for it — a PDA, which she knew was off-limits, but which I was willing to overlook just this once. Straightening back up, I noticed that Vanessa was watching with interest. In fact, her eyes were traveling over Cassie's curves in a way that I didn't appreciate. So I put both arms around Cassie and pulled her close, making it look as proprietary as possible. *Touch and die*, I told Vanessa silently.

She smirked and turned back toward the TV screen — but not before she ran a glance up and down me for good measure. Did Jenner know about this side of her? Was that what he saw in her? What *was* up with men? Not all men, surely, but almost all the ones *I* knew.

"You're thinking again," Cassie murmured.

"Sorry, sweetheart," I said.

On TV, Lisa Hartwell was live (at the time) in the Channel 12 newsroom, looking nervous. She was saying something about being sorry for the shock value of the footage, but news was news, and viewers could draw their own conclusions. Once again, I smiled wolfishly, noticing the big gestures she kept making with her left hand. She hadn't had that engagement ring before, and she obviously hadn't taken the time to borrow one that fit.

There was a quick cut back to the anchor desk, where Jim and Marilyn were wearing their most serious Serious News faces. "Lisa," Jim said somberly, "you were very brave to allow us to see that film. Thank you."

"You're welcome, Jim. It was a personally difficult decision, but I think the story isn't complete without it."

After that the tape ran out, and everyone except Cassie turned to look at me.

"There's so much wrong with that," I said, "that I don't even know where to start. But I hope you all noticed one thing ..."

"The fake engagement ring?" Heather asked. "Or the 'personally difficult decision'?"

"No. Notice where she was when she did the last segment. If it had been a real story, she'd have been sitting at the anchor desk with her dear friends Jim and Marilyn. But they had her on a live feed from the newsroom."

"I'm not following this," Chip said.

"Channel 12 wants it both ways," I explained. "They want the shock value, but they also want some distance from it. Lisa Hartwell doesn't know it yet, but she's on trial, too."

Chip groaned and rubbed his eyes. "Dev, I'm sorry, but I'm still —"

"All right, try it this way. The pot called the kettle black, but the pot was going to kiss the kettle back anyway, which is why the pot got stuck in the newsroom, waving an engagement ring around. It wasn't *really* a kiss. But it was on TV in front of God and everybody, so it must be true. This is going to be very, very embarrassing for the pot."

"What about the kettle?" Troy asked, grinning.

"The kettle gets to have some fun now."

"Not too much," Cassie snapped, squirming out of my grasp.

Amused, I let her go and then leaned back against the wall, surveying the room. "There's an old story about LBJ. Back when he was just another Texas politician, he was in a tight race, so he told his staff to start a rumor about his opponent. One of them said, 'Nobody's going to believe he's a pig fucker, Lyndon.' But LBJ said, 'I don't care if they believe it. I just want to make the pig fucker deny it.' "

Laughter, even from Vanessa, after the squirrel made a few extra circuits on the wheel that ran her brain.

"I'm done denying things," I said. "It's time to make someone else do it."

"How?" Vanessa asked.

"That's your job. You're in charge of the diversity campaign, aren't you? What did Jack call it — 'Rainbows for Peace'?"

Vanessa thought about it. "I'll have to talk to Mr. Jenner. But we can do this, I guess. If you tell me what you want, Devlin, I think I can help you. What should I tell him?"

"I'm glad you asked," I said, reaching over to grab a paper off my desk. "I have a little press release here. Just a draft, but see what he thinks."

She took it, read it two or three times and nodded. Then she gestured at Cassie. "What about her?"

Cassie glowered at Vanessa and moved a little closer to me.

"What about her?"

"You're going to drag her through this if you fight them," Vanessa said. "People are going to talk. People aren't stupid."

An extraordinary statement, considering the source. She couldn't possibly be as dumb as she seemed sometimes, and I didn't know whether that would help or hurt in the long run. But until I found out for sure, I was sticking with Plan A. "I want them to talk. Like Jenner always says, talk's good for business. But don't worry about Cassie; I'm not dragging her anywhere. When this is over, I'm resigning, and she stays —"

"Stop it, Devvy," Cassie said. "Wherever you go, we go together."

An even more extraordinary statement. We were obviously going to have to argue about everything all over again. Not now, though. "Maybe you should go see if Jenner's here," I said to Vanessa. "Take Kurt with you, if he's in."

She got up, clutching the paper. "I will. I'll tell you what happens."

"Good. Take notes, if you think of it."

She said she would, and we all watched her leave. No one said a word until the click of her heels faded on the other side of the door. Then Troy let out a long breath. "I don't trust her. She'll rat us out if she finds out what we're up to. ... What *are* we up to, anyway?"

I tried to look innocent. "We're not up to anything. We're just advertising diversity. You believe in diversity, don't you?"

"Sure I do," Troy said a little too loudly. "What do you want us to do?"

"Nothing you won't enjoy doing. But you can always tell people later that I made you do it."

"I thought the devil was the one who made people do things."

Heather laughed. "Satan, Dev — same difference."

"Same difference," I agreed. "Here's the plan."

Chapter Fourteen

Mid-November

It was almost too easy. The fish were all in the barrel, and even a child with a cap gun could take them out now with one shot. But I was a grown-up with much better weapons, content to watch and wait for the time being. There was no hurry, and as I'd always heard, watching fish *did* help lower a person's blood pressure.

There was nothing especially devious about the plan on its face. It was all in the press release: J/J/G would have no further comment on the Family Foundation thing, but it would have its own little public-service announcement soon. The agency was already working on it, for a client to be named later, and no agency in this market had ever done a PSA like this.

I'd known Jenner would go for that last part — he loved thinking of himself as a maverick — so it had been child's play to put the idea over the top.

"What we want," I'd told him, "is to wake the dead. Have you ever heard of Culture Club, Mr. Jenner?"

Seeing his face go blank, Vanessa had thought to be helpful. "It's a band, Nat. They were big a few years ago. You know — Boy George?"

"Never met him. Who's his lawyer?"

I'd been prepared for that. Rather than try to explain to Jenner what I wanted to do — much less who Boy George was, which could take days — I'd decided to show him. With J.B.'s help, I'd rough-cut a demo ad to "Church of the Poison Mind" that afternoon. So instead of answering the question in so many words, I'd simply played the tape and watched Jenner watch it.

"We can't do that on TV," he'd said — but with a faint question mark at the end of the sentence.

"We've already done it, sir. All the clips are from ads we've already run. They weren't cut this way, but anyone with a computer could do the same edits at home." That wasn't quite true — it would take a multimedia system and a person with way too much free time — but we weren't in the truth business anyway. "We can't use these clips again, but we can come as close as we want. I think we should shoot our own footage this time. Go for a cinéma vérité look."

Jenner had gone blank again. Before I could explain, though, Vanessa had jumped in. "Like home movies, or that tape of Devlin and

Cassandra."

I'd started to protest — but she was smirking at me much too knowingly. She was starting to trouble me in a serious way. What didn't I get about this woman?

Jenner hadn't really heard the last part, though; he'd just chewed on the cap end of his expensive fountain pen for a while. "Home movies. I like it. It's cheap. What about the song, Derry? Can we use it?"

"Too expensive for a PSA. But we'll get a jingle house to give us something along those lines. I'll have Kurt write the lyrics. That'll save us some money."

"Wheeler? Can he write lyrics?"

Sure, he could. Kurt was always writing parodies, usually when he was supposed to be writing ad copy. Officially, I didn't know about "Dev Is a Battlefield," but Cassie liked to sing it when she wanted to get my goat. "Yes, sir. He's got a knack for that kind of thing."

"I don't know, Derry. He isn't very mature, is he?"

"There are no old copywriters," I'd said, totally serious. "Besides, we don't want mature for this. If it doesn't shock people, we're not doing it right. You *do* want to stay out ahead of the competition, don't you? Say, Stu Bennett at Ad House?"

There'd been long silence in the office — so long that we could hear Sanchez on the phone outside, telling several callers in a row that Mr. Jenner was out of town again. Bennett was Jenner's bête noire, having wooed a series of very young women away from him over the years. Right now Jenner was still sulking about the loss of the Hardware City girl.

Pressing my luck, I'd continued. "His people did a piece of work on that last spot for WKKK, don't you think? I *personally* would never have dressed the DJ's up in sheets for a client with *those* call letters, but ..."

"All right," he'd said abruptly. "Get started. Let me see something in two weeks. You can go, Derry. Miss Vanessa, please stay."

I'd given her a meaningful look, which she'd returned. That much, at least, she understood. Then I'd headed for the door, already thinking about how I was going to work Kurt.

"Derry?"

"Sir?"

"You're sure this'll kill that bastard Bennett?"

"As dead as Nixon," I'd assured him.

"Then spend all the money you need. Have a good day."

I *had* had a good day, actually. Kurt was no challenge at all; he loved the idea. Jack didn't want to be bothered with the details. Vanessa was closeted with Jenner for the rest of the day; *I* didn't want to be bothered with *those* details. And Cassie, who didn't approve, was out of the way, off seeing clients. It took five minutes to call Heather, Troy and Chip in, issue them camcorders and tell them to have fun. They understood.

I wondered whether this was how Monica felt when she toyed with me ... and dismissed the thought. This was different. They'd asked for it.

∞ ∞ ∞

The Monday of the week before Thanksgiving, I went into the office early to get caught up on some work. Nothing unusual about that. No surprise, either, when Cassie let herself in. We hadn't seen each other since Sunday morning, and it was curious how often we both got to work early the morning after a night apart. Convenient, too, that we both had offices that locked — and duplicate keys.

"Do you have an appointment?" I asked, watching her relock the door.

"Do I need one?"

"Depends. What do you want?"

She perched on the arm of my chair, close enough to touch, but not touching yet. "What can I have?"

"I hate these kinds of conversations," I complained. "Out with it."

"You're a hard case, Kerry. My last three boyfriends would've kissed me hello by now."

"Your last three boyfriends would've been smoking a cigarette by now." Not that I didn't understand. She was wearing a perfectly proper business suit, but the blouse was half-open at the moment. The way she was sitting hiked the skirt way up; and not looking didn't help, as close as she was. "Sometimes I wonder if I should be insulted that you're with me. You always had terrible taste in men."

Cassie just laughed and leaned over to kiss me. After a few seconds of that, I pulled her the rest of the way down, and she pressed all the way in. My father had been right; it *did* pay to be nice to your co-workers.

"Damn you, Devvy," she murmured, "I just wanted a kiss hello. Now I won't get any work done all day."

"You're welcome."

"Yeah, well, same to you." Reluctantly, she got up, moving to the edge of my desk, and started rebuttoning her blouse. "We'll finish this later. I wanted to talk to you about something."

"What about?"

"Thanksgiving."

"What about Thanksgiving?"

"It's a week from Thursday."

"It's always on a Thursday. So?"

"Be serious for a minute. I talked to my mother last night."

"And ...?"

"I mean, I *talked* to my mother last night." She waited expectantly.

"Got that part the first time. And ...?"

"You're not following this, are you?"

"No," I admitted. "But if you hum a few bars ..."

Cassie drew a long breath. "She wanted to know when I'm coming home for Thanksgiving. I said I'd have to ask you. So she asked why you, and I said —"

Uh-oh. "You mean you *talked* to your mother?"

"She's my mother. I wasn't going to lie to her."

Well, why in hell not? Grimly, I remembered the last time the Wolfes had been in town. There'd been a two-hour lunch at which Mr. Wolfe had kept ordering wine, and somehow, there'd been a misunderstanding between him and me about Cassie's virginity. I hadn't meant to laugh when he brought it up — how was I supposed to know that he still believed in it? — and Cassie had defended me like a lioness, but lunch went straight downhill from there. Mrs. Wolfe had practically turned into a pillar of salt. I was never so glad to see two people get on a plane back to Kansas City.

"If you're thinking about that lunch," she said, "forget it. I straightened it out with them later. I *told* you that."

"Well, if you talked to your mother last night, you just unstraightened everything all over again. Do me a favor? The next time they're coming to town, let me know so I can get a good head start. Your dad's going to kill me for this, for sure, if he ever catches me."

"He's not going to kill you. I made Mom promise."

"Of course she promised. She wants the kill for herself," I grumbled.

"Let me finish. It's all right. They sort of knew, anyway."

Damn. I suddenly wondered whether *my* parents sort of knew. If they did, I was dead four times over, because *they* were going to kill me, too.

"Devvy?"

"What?"

"Mom wants you to come home with me for Thanksgiving."

"Out of the question."

"It's not that far. We might still be able to get a cheap flight."

"That's not the problem."

"You can stay in one of the guest rooms, if you'd feel better about it. You probably won't like my bedroom anyway. It's kind of pink." She frowned. "Come to think of it, I don't like it much either. Maybe I'll stay in *your* room."

"What room doesn't matter. Who's in it does. Were you planning to sleep with me?"

She gave me the not-even-you-can-be-that-stupid look.

"That's the problem," I said.

"I don't see why. They already know how it is with us."

"I know a lot more about how it is with us than they do. I've *been* there. And I'm not going to be a party to *that* at your parents' house. What if they got the wrong idea and called 911?"

Cassie considered that possibility. "No problem. We'll stay at a hotel."

"That would look bad. Forget it, Cass — I'm not going. Tell your mother I appreciate the invitation, but —"

"Then you call her and tell her yourself. I told her you'd be there."

Coolly, I regarded the stubborn woman parked on the edge of my desk. Lord knew I loved her, but she lost her mind like this sometimes. "When did I give you power of attorney?"

"I think it's more like custody. The witch handed you over to me." When I didn't bite, she looked disappointed. "All right, maybe I shouldn't have promised without talking to you first. But I really wish you'd come with me."

Suddenly, I got it. "Afraid of facing your family alone?"

"Something like that."

"You didn't have to tell them, you know. As far as that goes, you don't even have to go yourself. Would you rather come home with me? Spend Thanksgiving with my family?"

"God, no," Cassie said instantly. "Your family scares me."

I smiled faintly. "They scare me, too."

"You're not going to tell them, are you?"

"No."

"There's something wrong with that. Remind me to have a big fight with you about it soon. But I suppose we don't have to tell them right away."

"Or ever."

A few seconds' silence. "What about Christmas?"

"Drop it," I warned.

"Oh, all right." With an elaborate sigh, she slid off the desk and returned to the arm of my chair. "What's your day look like? Can you get away early?"

Hopefully, I paged through my planner. Like most days, this one was filled up and double-booked — and I had a private meeting with

Heather, Troy and Chip at 5:00 about the PSA. When it came to the fine points of the plan, what Cassie didn't know wouldn't hurt me. Then again, neither would an extra hour or two with her tonight. "What did you have in mind?"

"Well ..." She maneuvered herself onto my lap and got closer than strictly necessary; then she whispered her suggestion. Had she not been sitting there, I would've shot straight up into the air.

"Seriously?"

"After you call my mother, of course, and talk to her about Thanksgiving."

Half-annoyed, I pulled away. "Not even a nice try, Cass. I'm not that easy."

"Uh-huh," she said dryly ... and then caused me to grip the arms of my chair for dear life. She never *had* fought fair. I had a terrible feeling I was going to Kansas City.

Chapter Fifteen

As soon as Cassie left, I got busy rescheduling the day. Except for the Tom's Country Catering thing — lunch for the team, as a partial tradeout for our services — nothing couldn't wait. But I still wanted to see the team privately; we had some work to do before Jenner saw the first cut of the PSA on Friday.

A few minutes after I sent the group voice mail moving up the meeting, Kurt sauntered into my office, looking very pleased with himself. "It's not time yet," I informed him. "Come back when Mickey's little hand is on the three."

He just smiled and made himself at home in a guest chair.

"Kurt, I've got enough alligators in the swamp this morning. What do you want?"

"Nothing special. I know something, but if you're not interested, well ..." Knowing that it would tick me off, he tilted the chair back and put his feet up on the edge of the desk. "What do you think of Vanessa, boss? Pretty hot stuff, wouldn't you say?"

"I wouldn't. Is there a point to this conversation?"

"Only if you want to know what I know about her."

"If this is about sex —"

"Of course it's about sex. Want to know?"

Sometimes I hated being human. Did other species gossip? Poodles, maybe — I wouldn't put anything past a poodle — or possibly chickens. My Grandmother Whitaker had always sworn that chickens were the stupidest creatures on earth, next to my cousin Eddie. Last I'd heard, Eddie was driving a truck for some chicken operation down South, which had a certain poetry to it, as we'd all agreed last Christmas. He was on his fourth wife now, which we'd also agreed was a touch excessive, if not —

Dammit. I hated being a hypocrite, too. "All right, Kurt. Twenty-five words or less, and then get out of here."

"I can tell you in less than ten. She just made a pass at Connie the Barbarian."

Well, that *was* news. I wasn't sure why, but I didn't like it. "You've been working on this PSA, son. You're probably starting to see things. It happens. The whole time I worked on Rumours ..." Just in time, I caught myself. "It's an occupational hazard. Besides, you're wrong. She's sleeping with Jenner."

"No law against a girl batting for both teams. Look at you and

Cassie. Who'd have thought you two could switch-hit? Well, *her*, anyway."

"You leave Cassie out of this." Hating myself, I fought and lost a short battle not to ask the next question. "What did you see?"

"They were in the hall down by Jack's office. The babe was getting some mail off the mail cart, and she blew the dyke a kiss."

"That's not exactly a pass."

"Then the dyke gave her a big wet one right on the lips."

Abruptly, I set my coffee mug down with both hands. "That's enough. Go away. Go do some work, for a change. Don't come back until —"

"She didn't look like she minded much. Kind of too bad, you know, boss? I just lost $50 to Walt."

"For what?"

"We thought Vanessa was after you."

I gave him a very severe look. "Out."

"So it *is* kind of too bad. We had another $100 on how many pieces she'd be in when Cassie found out. I was down for microscopic."

"*Now.*"

"There's still one thing we can't figure out, though. What do you suppose Cassie sees in you? Can't be your looks. Nothing personal, boss, but —"

"It's my charm," I growled. "*Now get out.*"

He laughed and took his time getting back on his feet. "Always a pleasure. *Auf Wiedersehen*, Dev. Don't let the Barbarians bite."

I watched him leave to make sure he was gone; then I watched the closed door for a while to make sure he didn't come back. Vanessa and the Barbarian? If I were still in junior high, I would have said ick. But maybe there was nothing wrong with saying it now; the ick factor *was* awfully high.

Someone tapped on the door again. Not Kurt's knock — he went for that macho jamb-rattling thing — and not anyone else's I recognized. "Who is it?"

The door opened, and I leaped like a guilty lizard. The Barbarian didn't appear to notice, though. "Morning, Kerry. Got some FedEx for you."

I mumbled something and tried to look busy while she tossed the envelope into my inbox. When she didn't go away right away, I looked up — a mistake, because she was standing close enough now for me to see the lipstick smears. Only Vanessa wore lipstick that red, which meant that Kurt had told the truth.

Ick.

The Barbarian just grinned and reached into a back pocket for a bandanna. "Oops. Guess I forgot to clean up after. You wanna borrow this?"

"Why?" I asked, wincing as she spat into the bandanna.

"Oh, no reason. No reason." She spat again and started scrubbing her face. "Sure you don't wanna borrow it?"

"I'm sure." Damn Cassie anyway.

The Barbarian stuffed the bandanna back into her pocket and winked. Then she ambled out, whistling "I Enjoy Being a Girl."

I waited till my blood pressure dropped a few points and then dug some Kleenex out of a desk drawer. The Barbarian was on my list now, too.

∞ ∞ ∞

The smell of cooking started around 11:00 and grew stronger the closer it got to noon. By the time I got to the conference-room wing, a crowd was loitering outside room A, looking hungry.

"One side," I said, pushing one of the smaller account execs out of the way.

"What's going on in there, Dev?" someone asked. "I thought there was a meeting."

"There is. Don't make me late."

"But it smells like food. Is somebody grilling something in there?"

"The client."

"You're grilling the client?"

I didn't have time for this. "We had no choice. He was a problem. We think he'll be fine with a little mango chutney on the side, though. Now move. I'm late for lunch."

Sometimes my reputation was a good thing. No one was sure whether to believe me, but no one wanted to take any chances. In a matter of seconds, the hall was as empty as a pyramid. Rather satisfied with the result, I pushed open the conference-room door.

At first, my brain simply refused to process the scene. There really *was* grilling going on in there. The client had a portable rotisserie set up at one end of the conference table, with a suckling pig turning on a spit over open flame — good for at least one violation of city ordinances and probably a huge rent increase if the building owner ever found out. My colleagues were all pressed against the walls, as far from the flames as possible.

Warily, I opened the closet door to see whether the fire extinguisher was still inside. It was. So was Jenner. He had a white-knuckle grip on the extinguisher and refused to let go.

"You won't be any safer in there, sir," I said to him.

"I can't be aware of this, Derry. Not officially. Harper said so. Close the door. Call me when lunch is ready."

He was the boss. Shrugging, I shut the door. "Jack?"

"Kerry?"

"Do I want to know why the smoke alarms aren't going off?"

"No."

All right, then. If there was nothing I could do, there was nothing I could do. Cassie, no fool, was over by the window; I decided to join her. "Afternoon, Cass. Nice day. How have you been? Family okay?"

She pulled me closer, but only to jab an elbow in my ribs.

"What was that for?"

"You know *exactly* what that's for. We're roasting Babe on a spit in a conference room, and you're just standing there letting it happen."

"It's a little late to stop it. The pig's almost done."

"You could make them stop if you wanted to."

Kurt and Chip were listening intently; I shot them a look that made them step back. Then I pulled Cassie a little closer to the window. "Sweetheart, they're all crazy. If there were flamingoes in here, they'd all be playing croquet."

"This isn't Wonderland."

True, but irrelevant. "It doesn't matter. When in Rome, Cass. You know that."

"I know that. I don't have to like it."

"But you like commissions," I said encouragingly. "You like roasted pigs, too."

She debated whether to prolong the sulk and finally decided against it. "That had better not be poi in that dish. I hate poi."

"That's the spirit. Hungry now?"

"Starved."

Checking first to make sure the coast was clear, I gave her a discreet little kiss on the top of her head. "It'll work out, Cass. Trust me. By the time I'm done with them, they'll only wish *they* were on that spit."

She gave me an indiscreet little hug and held on. "Promise?"

"Promise."

"Devvy?"

"Hmm?"

"This doesn't let you off the hook for Thanksgiving."

As gently as possible, I wrenched the woman off. We would do this later. Right now, we were going to have pig with the Romans.

∞ ∞ ∞

By the time we finished lunch — and Jenner, Jack and the client stepped out to smoke cigars — the pig was only a memory and a pile of bones, one of which Kurt was still sucking. "Marrow," he explained when I told him to stop it.

Vanessa, who'd only picked at a tiny portion of salad all through lunch, looked interested for the first time all day. The next thing I knew, she was sucking on a bone, too, in a very different way ... and so was Troy. It was truly revolting, like show-and-tell by sex offenders.

Then something struck me. Heather had her camcorder with her; she'd gotten so far into the spirit of the thing that she'd been taking it everywhere. So I got up and tapped her on the shoulder. "Borrow your camera?"

Busy keeping Troy and Vanessa under minute surveillance, she handed it over without even looking up. To get a better angle, I walked around the table — which meant passing Cassie, who grabbed the tail of my jacket.

"Make sure you get Vanessa's bad side," she whispered.

Pretending not to have heard that, I turned on the camera and started shooting, knowing it would only make things worse. Kurt actually jammed a bone up his nose to get extra lens time. Likewise, Troy and Vanessa amped up their acts even more when the red light went on. Without comment, I kept filming.

"They're being disgusting," Heather spat. "Why are you putting this on tape?"

"Christmas-party reel," I lied.

"I don't trust you, Dev."

A very smart girl. I just kept the camera rolling.

∞ ∞ ∞

That night Cassie and I had Greek pizza and a few shots of ouzo while we ran rough cuts of the PSA. I didn't like ouzo, but she'd put the bottle in the freezer overnight, and the cold seemed to have killed some of the taste. By the second shot, it didn't really matter.

"Either I'm looped," she said, "or I've seen this one before."

"You have. You made me rewind it four times."

"Did I?" She looked only vaguely surprised. "Well, you know how I love your work, pookie."

"Don't call me 'pookie.' And it isn't *my* work. Not yet. What do you think so far?"

"I think it's missing something. I don't know what, exactly."

"Try this," I said, reaching over for my attaché and pulling out the tape I'd shot that afternoon.

She grumbled about having to get off the couch, but she got to the VCR and back without damage. Then she octopused herself around me, "to be friendly," she explained.

"That's one word for it."

"Just run the tape. After that you can call my mother, and then I'll give you that little treat I promised."

Hmm. She'd had more ouzo than I had; maybe one more shot would make her forget the part about her mother. The trick was to make it a small shot, so she wouldn't forget the part about the treat, too. While I calculated the half-life of ouzo, I started the tape with one hand.

At first nothing seemed unusual. Yes, Kurt had that bone up his nose, but content aside, the tape looked fine. Troy and Vanessa's little display had come out nicely, too.

"That's *so* disturbing," Cassie said. "Play it again."

I ran the tape back, this time in slow motion. "See this part? I might zoom in during editing, to —"

"Stop it," she said abruptly, sitting up straight.

"No. This is the whole point. I want —"

"The tape, I mean. Stop it."

"Something wrong?"

"I don't know. Let me have the remote a second."

Shrugging, I stopped the tape and handed her the remote. She rewound a short way and then punched a button.

"There. See that?"

"Vanessa and Troy. So?"

"Look at her eyes, Devvy."

I squinted a bit, the better to see. "Red-eye. I must've pointed the light wrong. Well, no problem — I'll take it out in editing."

"It's not red-eye. Look at Troy. He's in the same frame."

"Then it must've been some weird angle on her. What's the difference? I'm going to run this tape through so many computer programs that its own mother won't know it. It'll just take a second to get rid of —"

"It's not red-eye. Go look."

I didn't see any point, but was all for keeping her happy, so I went over to the TV and bent down close to the screen.

Then I saw. "Damn. Damn. *Damn.*"

"I wonder whether we can get a group discount on exorcists," Cassie said.

Chapter Sixteen

Very Early Tuesday

When I was sure Cassie was asleep, I carefully separated from her and climbed out of bed. She didn't stir until I covered her back up, and then only to steal all the covers. It figured. Sleeping with her had many compensations, but half the blankets wasn't one of them.

As quietly as possible, I put on my pajamas and last night's shoes and kissed the top of her blonde head, which was all I could find of her in that mountain of bedding. Then I prowled the upstairs, looking for the way to the attic. Something had been drawing me there for the past few hours, ever since I'd seen those eyes on that videotape, and something told me that thing was Monica. I hadn't mentioned it to Cassie, because she wouldn't want to know. Besides, that last ouzo had worked like a charm; she'd forgotten about making me call her mother. Why ruin what had turned out to be a very fine evening after all?

So I would go alone to see what Monica wanted. First, though, I had to figure out how to get up to the attic. Cassie had said something once about a fold-down ladder in a very inconvenient place ...

Eventually, I found it — a panel in the ceiling of a walk-in closet in the guest bedroom. Grumbling under my breath, I found a pole with a hook on it at the back of the closet, used it to grab the brass ring on the ladder panel and pulled. The panel squeaked enough that it might wake her up; I left the hook pole dangling from the ring while I went back to close her bedroom door.

When I came back, the ladder was already folded down, and a light was on in the attic.

"Monica?" I whispered.

No answering sound except for a faint patter on the roof. Cautiously, I climbed the first three rungs of the ladder and felt a cool breeze that smelled like rain. Great. Apparently a window was open up there, and it had been raining all night. No doubt Monica was out to ruin Cassie's house, too. I would've thought she would've gone in for Amityville Horror tricks — green slime or blood running down the walls — but Cassie would be just as furious about rainwater.

Briefly, I considered the options: face a demon in the attic or face my beloved if I didn't go up and close the window. *That* was a no-brainer. I went on up the ladder.

The attic was clear of demons at first glance. Anything could be hiding behind all those boxes and trunks, of course, but Monica wasn't the hiding type. Oddly, too, both windows were closed. But the wind and the smell of rain were coming from somewhere else, somewhere in the ceiling, through no opening that I could see ...

At which point a mouse ran over my shoe, and I rather lost track of things for a minute. It wasn't that I was scared of mice. One of my best friends in grade school had a pet white rat, and he'd been harmless enough, even when we dressed him up in Barbie clothes. But an unexpected mouse was a whole other story. I did a little dance; it made a little squeak; then it scurried between two boxes, out of sight.

I took a moment to recover my wits, feeling stupid but keeping sharp watch on the place where I'd last seen the mouse. Cassie hated all mice indiscriminately, and she would send me back with a carving knife if she ever found out. Maybe I'd get Kurt to do it instead. He could probably reason with the creature on its own level, rodent to rodent.

Speaking of creatures, I still had to deal with Monica. Pushing the mouse to the back of my mind, I started to search the attic again — and found another fold-down ladder folded down from the ceiling, the night sky clearly visible through the opening that hadn't been there before.

That was a demon for you. She could've just yanked me out of bed again, but no — now I had to climb up to the roof to talk with her. Well, *I* wanted to talk with *her* about that. Goaded, I went up the ladder and pulled myself onto the roof.

No Monica. Was she hiding behind the chimney? Hanging upside down from a branch of the walnut tree? I hated it when she got cute.

"Monica? Damn you, where are you?"

I was about to check the other chimney when a hand touched my shoulder. Startled, I turned — faster than a smart person would turn on slippery roof shingles.

Vanessa barely caught me in time. With no effort at all, she set me back on my feet and then shook her head in dry amusement. "You should know better than to go up on a roof in the rain in those shoes. Try something with a little tread next time. Did you know Nordstrom has a cute little ankle boot that —"

"You!"

"You sound surprised."

"Surprised, hell — I'm *mad.* I climb halfway up Kilamanjaro, in the rain, looking for Monica, and I get *you?*"

"You don't want to talk about shoes?"

Breathing hard, trying to control my temper, I gave her a narrow once-over. She was wearing the same kind of black gown Monica always wore, and there was just enough streetlight for me to see her eyes, which were the same weird shade of red. This was a trick, of course. Monica was probably shape-shifting again. I'd never quite forgiven her for turning into Cassie on me that night last summer. But if she thought I was going to fall for that trick twice, with Vanessa of all people ...

"I'm not Monica," she said. "God, don't insult me."

"If you're reading my mind, read a little farther. I've thought a lot worse of you."

"Of course you have. But that's not important. It's time we had a talk, Devlin."

"Fine. We can talk inside. I'll get Cassie, and then —"

"Not just yet. It's a beautiful night. I thought a little fresh air would do you good. You like rain, don't you?"

"That's not the point. The point is ..." I wished I'd learn to stop saying that; it was one of those sentences I never seemed to know how to finish. "Quit yanking my chain, Monica. I know you're in there. Show yourself."

"Really, Devlin. Isn't enough of me showing already?" A flash of fangs in the streetlight, which might have been a smile. "They warn us about this in Demon Ed. Let a celibate loose just once, and you'll never —"

"Cut that *out.* How stupid do you think I am? Demon Ed?"

She reached into the front of her gown — an action that I made a point of not watching. When I looked again, she was handing me a small pamphlet. It was exactly the size, shape and design of those little tracts the street preachers passed out downtown, an irony that would have amused me more had I not been in a temper. The last time I'd run into one of those yahoos —

"You and Cassie decided to walk to lunch that day," Vanessa said matter-of-factly, "and you had to go across Mad Mac's corner. That was before the city got hold of him and made him get a storefront, of course. He was oppressing some poor old woman about how Jesus loved her, at the top of his lungs, so you gave him one of those looks of yours ..."

My blood froze. "How do you *know* that?"

"... and you didn't think he saw, but he had eyes in the back of his head, because he turned around and looked right at you ..."

"We didn't tell anyone about that. It was too stupid to even mention. So how do you —"

"... and he said, 'But Jesus doesn't love *you.*' Cassie tried to bop him with her purse. I know you remember this, Devlin."

Dead silence on the roof, except for the rain and the rustling of bare branches in the wind. She was right — and she wasn't Monica, either. Monica would have had a few choice comments about my carrying Mad Mac's words around all these years. Vanessa just stated the fact, without malice.

"It's too bad your parents are Methodists," she said. "If you'd been brought up Catholic, you'd have lapsed a long time ago, and you'd have just popped the little twerp one. You really *should* be an ex-Catholic, you know. All that Irish blood ..." Another flash of fangs. "Oh, well. We win some; we lose some. Read the little book."

"In the dark?"

"Oh." She reached back into her gown and came up with a lighted candle. "Here."

It was a good thing that I was used to this sort of thing by now. Without comment, I took the candle and held it close to the pamphlet. The title was in Russian, which might as well have been Greek or Sanskrit for all the good it did.

"Mikhail Bulgakov wrote some of it," she explained. "With Gogol. C.S. Lewis has a beer with them every now and then. They —"

That wasn't funny. *"Stop that right now."*

"You're forgetting *The Screwtape Letters.* C.S. got it all backward, but he did get it."

Annoyed, I lighted the pamphlet with the candle and then threw both burning things into the rain as hard as I could. "Give me one good reason not to throw you off this roof, Vanessa."

"Hmm. That's a toughie." She put her fingertip to her temple and frowned in a mock show of deep thinking — and I had to blink hard, because for just a second, she turned into a Valley Girl with big hair and see-through pink clothes. It was getting so hard to tell anymore whether I was losing my mind. "One good reason? It would mess up my dress. This thing takes forever to dry."

"I've got time," I informed her, taking a menacing step in her direction.

"Want one more reason?"

I kept moving. "No. I want to throw you off the roof."

"You don't want to hurt me. I'm Cassandra's demon."

Outraged, I completely lost my balance. Vanessa grabbed me again.

"Say that one more time," I demanded.

"I'm Cassandra's demon."

With all the force I could command, I threw her off the roof. Then, dusting my hands off, I went back down the ladder to the attic.

Where Vanessa was standing, unharmed and whole, with a tolerant little smile on her face.

"Can't blame me for trying," I said.

"It won't work on Monica, either."

"Am I asleep, by any chance? I have crazy dreams sometimes.

Maybe it was the ouzo."

"You're awake."

That was what I was afraid of. "Does Cassie know?"

"Not yet. Go wake her up, and we'll tell her. I'll meet you downstairs."

I nodded and started to fold the ladder back into the ceiling. While I did, she stuck something small and flat into my pajama pocket. "Tracts don't burn," she explained.

"Demon Ed," I said heavily. "By Bulgakov and Gogol. In Russian."

"Well, not all of it. C.S. Lewis wrote the captions."

Of course he did. I'd just been up on the roof, in the rain, in my pajamas, in the middle of the night, in an expensive part of Greenville, with a co-worker who said she was a demon — and not just any demon, but Cassie's. Two dead Russians and a dead Brit were writing tracts in some corner pub in hell, laughing like madmen, and Mad Mac was playing touch football with Howard Abner at a cheap motel in Blue Valley, both of them in prom dresses. Sure. Why not?

I watched my mind slip its moorings and drift through the opening in the ceiling, between the branches of the walnut tree and on out into the night, as bright in the dark sky as a red balloon. It might have been my imagination, but the balloon seemed to be wearing a pair of tiny horns.

∞ ∞ ∞

Cassie made another circle of the living room, scowling, arms folded, not happy. She'd been unhappy enough when I woke her up — I'd forgotten that I was dripping, that the rain had been cold and that she wasn't wearing a thing — and when she'd gotten over being dripped on, she'd had a second fit because I was standing there in wet pajamas and soggy shoes. In no mood for explanations, she'd dragged me to her peach-and-blue bath by the ear, stripped everything off and turned her hair dryer on stun. It was an interesting situation, but I was pretty well immune to interesting by now, and being blow-dried by a blonde in her birthday suit was just one more thing.

She hadn't liked hearing that Vanessa was downstairs, either, when I finally got a word in edgewise. She complained about it the whole time we were getting dressed, and she practically bit Vanessa's head off when we got down to the living room. But Vanessa had simply smiled and pointed at the fireplace, which instantly roared to life, shutting Cassie up for a second. That was long enough for me to get her settled on the couch and to get a good grip on her while Vanessa told her who she was.

That had been half an hour ago. Cassie was relatively calm now, and

Vanessa was still talking. It had been a lot of nonsense, really, about demons and angels and gods, and how humans got them all confused, but she'd promised at the start to keep Monica away if we agreed to listen, and that had been good enough for Cassie.

For my part, I'd been leaning against the wall for a while, sipping brandy and trying not to think. Cassie had thrown down her own brandy in one shot and refused a refill; she'd been pacing a hole in the carpet ever since.

Vanessa didn't seem to mind. She just kept talking about guardian demons and competition for souls and Monica's eternal propensity to cheat. It seemed that there'd been a bet between them about Cassie and me. Monica thought she could get my soul the old-fashioned way — with guilt, temptation and sex, not necessarily in that order. Vanessa said she was crazy, because Cassie would be better at the sex part than Monica was, having Vanessa as her demon and all. There'd been a big argument about that, with many rude things said, all of which Vanessa repeated with venom ... and it was all starting to give me a headache. There was a bottle of Advil in the bath upstairs; I decided to go take a few and then have another brandy.

But Cassie cut me off, informing me that I wasn't leaving the room. She meant business, by the look in her eye, so I decided to go hold up the wall some more.

Finally, Vanessa finished. It was quiet for a long time except for the scuff of Cassie's flats on the carpet as she continued to pace.

"Questions?" Vanessa asked.

Cassie gave her a terrible look, but kept her own counsel.

"Devlin? Questions?"

"Cassie's not happy," I said. "I don't think she likes having a demon. Any chance you could just go away?"

"I could, if you really want." Vanessa examined her talons under the lamplight, looking bored. "But then Monica would have a clear field, and she'd finish you off. It's nothing to *me*, of course, but Cassie would miss you, and we'd have to start sleeping with salesmen again."

I didn't like the sound of that one bit and scowled at Cassie preemptively. She scowled right back.

"That's the problem when demons compete," Vanessa said. "The winner can send the loser back inside. I don't want to get back inside your girl, if you don't mind. She has terrible taste in men." Finding some imperfection in one nail, she reached into her gown for a file; I made a mental note to set up a purse concession when I got to hell. "I hate sleeping with salesmen. They are the absolute worst. No technique — just close, close, close. It's enough to make a demon weep."

"And if you win, and Monica loses ...?"

"*I* could send *her* back inside. That would be fun. You and Cassandra and Monica, all in the same bed —"

"Over my dead body," Cassie spat.

"But I won't," Vanessa said quickly. "Just because I'm a demon doesn't mean I'm evil. I'm on *your* side."

Cassie stopped cold in her tracks, and we both regarded her in silence.

"Oh, all right, all right, I'm evil. But Monica's worse. Believe me, you want me to win. I'll just drive her into a Junior Leaguer or something. No one would ever notice the difference." She swiped the file across her nails, smiling wickedly. "So. Are you with me?"

"What do you want us to do?" I asked.

"Nothing you won't enjoy doing."

Damn, that sounded familiar. It had been a setup when I'd said it, and I wasn't even a demon. Were we about to make a worse deal with a different devil?

Uncertain, I caught Cassie's eye. She beckoned me over.

"What do you think?" she whispered.

"She's your demon. It's your call."

"I don't trust her."

"Neither do I. But I trust you."

The look on her face was worth whatever this was going to cost me. "Thank you. I love you. I mean it. ... Vanessa?"

Being busy filing her claws, the demon didn't bother to glance up. "Cassandra?"

"About what you're going to do to Monica if you win."

"*When* I win," Vanessa corrected, still filing.

Cassie smiled slightly and reached for my hand. "Does it have to be a Junior Leaguer? Could you drive her into anyone?"

That got Vanessa's full attention — and mine. The demon laughed. "Go on."

"It was an academic question," Cassie lied. "I just wondered. But while I'm wondering ..."

"Yes. It can be arranged. Are you with me?"

"And Devvy and I stay together, no matter what?"

"Like I could keep you apart. Now, are you *with* me?"

"Yes," Cassie said. But what Vanessa couldn't see — and what I wouldn't have known had I not been holding her hand — was that she'd crossed her fingers.

∞ ∞ ∞

"That was a stupid trick, Cass."

"So? She's a dumb blonde." She sighed and snuggled a bit closer. "God, I hate demons. Yours is bad enough. But mine ..."

"She's not full-time dumb."

"She's sleeping with Jenner."

There was no winning that point, so I conceded it.

"You said you trust me," she said.

"I do. But I just think it's —"

"I think *your* plan is stupid, too. But I trust you."

"That may have been your first mistake," I admitted.

"You're trouble, all right, pookie. You're lucky I like trouble."

Irritably, I pushed her off and scooted to the far side of the bed.

"Babycakes?" she asked, amused. "Buttercup? Honeybunch?"

With maximum dignity under the circumstances, I grabbed all the covers and made a Porthault-and-goose-down fort around myself.

The mattress shifted as she started to crawl my way. "Bluebird? Bunny rabbit?"

Was she out of her mind? I scooted a little farther.

She was laughing now, the fiend. "Lamb chop? Chicken teriyaki?"

I gave the covers a mighty pull — and went over the edge. Cassie lost it, laughing so hard that she almost got hiccups.

"I meant to do that," I snarled.

She composed herself with great effort. "Of course you did, pookie." Then she lost it again.

And this was the woman who was going to fight at my side against J/J/G, the Family Foundation, two thousand years of street preaching, pigheadedness in general, sexual pigheadedness in particular and two demons. I was in trouble.

Lucky I liked trouble, too.

Chapter Seventeen

Tuesday Morning

There was no excuse for not expecting it. Even though I hadn't slept all night, and even though I was starting to take the weirdest things for granted, I should have known what just had to be next. When I got to work in the morning, Monica was in my office, dressed up like a person. Well, make that a person in a very, very short skirt.

"You'll never guess," she said without preface, "so I'll tell you. I'm your new admin. You can call me Ms. Kerry. I told Mr. Jenner we're no relation — yet. Do you like my costume?"

Keeping a mistrustful eye on her, I hung up my raincoat and grabbed the biggest mug. She had, at least, made coffee.

"I scheduled you for an extra meeting this morning. I invited Kurt."

Without comment, I filled up the mug.

"I also called Mrs. Wolfe. You accepted her kind invitation. And I got you two seats to Kansas City on a *very* early flight next Wednesday."

Just to be safe, I topped it off.

"You don't look surprised to see me." Her tone was a bit petulant.

"Nothing surprises me anymore. I've got demons from here to the South Pole. What do you want now?"

"What I've always wanted. You're making it hard on me, Devlin. That's going to go very hard on *you.*" She showed me her fangs, by way of reminder that she kept them sharp. "But there'll be time for settling up. How do you feel about a thousand years of fire and then a thousand years of ice?"

Shrugging, I settled in at my desk and switched on the computer. "Not very original."

"I can do worse."

"I'm not afraid of Martha Stewart. Or polka music."

"Hell is diverse," Monica said ominously, pointing at the Mac, which was still booting up. All of a sudden, I had the Windows Blue Screen of Death.

"Cut that out."

"I thought you'd hate that. How about this?"

I started to tell her that any admin of mine had too much work to do to play games when movement on the screen caught my eye. It looked like streaming video of something. A football game, maybe? Out of habit, I moused down to where I kept the RealPlayer icon with the idea of making some adjustments on the picture.

"Allow me," Monica said.

The next thing I knew, what had been on the computer screen was a hologram in the middle of the office, complete with very loud audio. It was a football game, all right. Unseen people all around me were screaming in Southern at the big lunkheads lining up in front of my desk. Curious, I leaned over to check the carpet. The desk was right on the twenty-yard line. Not a bad seat.

"No popcorn?" I asked.

"Great Satan, you're getting jaded," she grumbled. "Just watch."

The noise was deafening. The quarterback in the red jersey turned to yell something to the backfield, but they couldn't hear a word; immediately, he called time out. As he straightened, I frowned; he looked awfully familiar.

Then the center reared back on its hind legs, and there was no question: It was Howard Abner. Howard Abner twenty years ago, maybe, but definitely one and the same. Not what I really wanted to ...

Wait a minute. The quarterback was Abner, too. So was the backfield. And so were all the lunkheads in yellow and white on the other side of the line.

"Not funny, Monica," I warned.

She laughed and strolled through one of the huddles — literally through it, like a ghost. Then she took a seat on the edge of my desk, the way Cassie did. "Wait till they start playing again."

I had a very bad feeling about this. "I think I know where this is going. Let's not go. It's very cute of you, but —"

"Shh," she said, leaning over to kiss the top of my head. It burned a little.

A referee's whistle drew my attention back to the field. Twenty-two Howard Abners squared off again, the crowd started howling again and this time the ball got snapped. At least, I'd thought it was a ball up to that point. But it was, in fact, a live pig, still using its skin, and it turned out to be irrelevant, because the quarterback heaved it toward the sideline — right at me. I barely ducked in time.

"It's all right. It's one of them, too," Monica explained.

"Not funny," I repeated.

She looked terribly pleased with herself. "Never said it was."

Where the hell was the close box on this thing? I tried to click the RealPlayer window on the computer screen, but nothing happened. Was it in a corner of the hologram? I got up to get a better look. Then I realized what was happening on the field.

"Make that *stop*, Monica."

"Why? Sauce for the goose isn't sauce for the gander?"

"But they're ... they're ... God!" I jumped out of the way just before an ardent linebacker tackled an equally ardent wide receiver. It was child's play to tell how they felt; nobody was wearing any pants anymore. The crowd was going wild. "Get me out of this picture. *Now.*"

"You used to be more fun," she complained.

"Things used to make sense. It was easier then."

"Was it?"

All right, maybe not, but at least it wasn't this messy. And I had never, *ever* had a gay Baptist orgy in my office before. "Just make it stop."

Monica didn't answer for a second; she seemed to be intrigued by something down by her feet. I glanced over — and instantly clapped both hands over my eyes.

"Oh, all right," she finally said. The noise stopped, and when it was safe to look again, I found the hologram gone, too. "Better, pookie?"

"Don't start with that, Monica. So that's your idea of hell?"

"Only one of them. One of yours, if we want to be accurate. Would you like to see the wedding reception with the Chicken Dance instead? ... No? I agree. That's a bad one. How about the all-Wayne Newton radio station? Or Thanksgiving with your father's side of the family?" She smiled unpleasantly. "*Next* year, of course. You're spending this one with the Wolfes."

"You can't have my soul. It's too late. I don't think Cassie wants to give it back anyway."

"You don't seriously think I'm afraid of her. Let alone that ... *imp* of hers."

"Vanessa? She says she's —"

"She's not big enough to be a demon. She's an imp. No — make that an *impette.*" Looking disgusted, she leaned over to speak confidentially. "*I* would *never* have kissed that Barbarian person, Devlin. She has hideous taste in men."

"Sounds familiar."

"Well, it should. Where do you think your Cassie got it from?"

"We probably shouldn't have this conversation."

"I miss you," she said suddenly. "What if I get rid of both of them? I could give you a couple hundred more years to surrender. We could have such fun. We *did* have fun. Remember?"

Yes, we had, and, yes, I did. But that was then, and this was ...

... going to get me killed if Cassie found out. "History," I said.

Monica leaned farther down, eyes glittering. There was a chance that I was in trouble. "Nobody knew then. Nobody has to know again.

No TV reporters, no lies to clients, no talk in the office ... I could turn Kurt into a possum, if you'd like. His little friend, Walt, too. I could arrange a possum wedding for them. A pity neither of them could wear white, but then, the rules may be different for possums. Would you like that?"

"Forget it, Monica. I already told you —"

"And Cassandra doesn't have to know, either. It'll be our secret." She stretched out a razor-sharp fingernail and ran it around my ear, just enough to draw blood.

"Damn it, that isn't going to w —"

Work. It wasn't going to work. Except that she was licking the blood off, and I'd somehow forgotten the word.

"No one will know," she murmured. "She was supposed to destroy you. In her way. She can still try. In her way. But I still know a few tricks that she doesn't. Remember?"

Damn. Now I understood what the word *diabolical* meant. "Get out of my office. I mean it."

"That's the last thing you mean." Monica slithered across the desk, putting certain parts of herself directly in my line of sight. "I think —"

The office door slammed open — and for the first and only time in my professional life, I was relieved. Cassie looked to be in a mood, and Vanessa, right behind her, looked to be in one, too. With some force, I pushed Monica aside. "It's not what you think, Cass. She —"

"Stay out of this, Devvy," Cassie commanded, glaring at Monica. "You. In the admin drag. Off the desk."

"She's trying to threaten me, Devvy," Monica remarked. "Isn't that cute?"

Even from a distance, I could clearly see the hot blue glint in Cassie's eyes. "Nobody calls her 'Devvy' but me. *Nobody.* Especially not *you*, you ... you ..."

"Let me," Vanessa said, rather happily. "Slut!" Then, with impossible speed, she yanked on Monica's designer jacket and hurled her to the carpet. "An impette, am I, Ms. Scarier-Than-Thou? An *impette?*"

This could get ugly. Not wasting a second, I shot out of my chair and pushed Cassie to the opposite wall. "Stay behind me. And don't say one more word."

"Let go, Devvy. I can take care of myself."

"That's what I'm afraid of," I said grimly, blocking her as best I could.

There was a howl of outrage from the carpet, followed by a thud. Cassie fought clear of my shoulder. "At least let me *see*."

With misgivings, I pulled back a little, but kept a tight hold on her.

Only when I was sure she wasn't going to make a break for it did I turn to see what was going on. Where the linebackers had been rolling around just minutes ago, now Monica and Vanessa were having at each other — with different intent but equal intensity. It was every cliché of a catfight, complete with shrieking and hair-pulling. The only difference was that every time one of them said a bad word, a patch of the carpet caught fire. Just from where I stood, I could see about half a dozen little blazes.

"Disturbing," Cassie said.

"Very."

"Fifty bucks says mine wins."

"This kind of talk is exactly what got us into this trouble in the first place," I reminded her.

"Don't like your odds, baby duck?"

I scowled at her. She smiled back sweetly, raised up on tiptoe and put a tiny kiss on the bridge of my nose.

"A little help here?" Vanessa yelled.

We turned again. Monica was jumping up and down on Vanessa's spine. That had to hurt, especially with *those* shoes.

"Raise you fifty," I said to Cassie.

"Done. No personal checks. Cash money."

I was starting to argue with that when the office door slammed open again. Oh, hell. Of all the wrong people to walk in at the wrong time ...

Cassie took one look and sank down on my shoulder. It was too late to worry how that looked — Lisa Hartwell from Channel 12 was in the doorway with a cameraman; the camera's red light was on. And Jenner, Jack and Kurt were right behind them. To their credit, they all seemed stunned.

Even Monica and Vanessa were surprised. But I suppose that even demons would have a hard time explaining how they came to be in this position this early in the morning on a work day. This sort of thing *just wasn't normal.*

"Do something," Cassie whispered.

Chapter Eighteen

"**Do something**," **Cassie had said**. I was at a loss to imagine what. Two demons were having a knock-down, drag-out in my office, which happened to be on fire, she was pretty much all over me and it was all exactly what it looked like.

Well, I'd *wanted* an interesting job.

"Is that fire?" the reporter asked in a tiny voice.

"Yes," I said.

She was trying hard not to see Cassie, I could tell; she was looking somewhere just over my head. "Shouldn't you do something about it?"

"I don't know. I kind of like it."

Cassie sighed, but made no move to disengage herself.

"Dammit, Kerry," Jack complained, "your *office* is on fire. This is going to come out of your paycheck." He shouldered the TV crew aside, grabbed the coffee carafe and nodded curtly at Monica and Vanessa. "Stand aside, ladies."

"They're not ladies," I said. "They're —"

"Administrative assistants," Kurt interrupted. "Darn pretty ones, too. Don't you think, Mr. Jenner?"

But Jenner was already gone. At the first sight of fire, he'd bolted.

Meanwhile, Jack was racing around the room, pouring coffee on everything that was burning. So much for that carpet.

Deliberately, I looked right into the lens of the TV camera. "We'll be sacrificing the virgins in a minute, Ms. Hartwell. Guess that lets *you* out."

"Let's not get personal," she said, suddenly bristling.

"I won't if you won't. But I'll bet you will." Against my better judgment, I let go of Cassie. "Want to tell us why you're here? Or is it a secret?"

"I'm following up on a tip. My editor wants —"

"Ratings? Well, of course he does. Nice engagement ring, by the way. It fits a lot better than the other fake one. How much did it set you back?"

Caught, she flushed pink. "It isn't —"

"Good choice. Zirconium is getting really affordable. And just think — you'll already have the ring when you meet Mr. Right. Or ..." Something made me look over at Monica. She was smiling evilly, just the tips of her fangs visible. "Maybe Ms. Right. A person can never be too sure these days."

Jack, still putting out fires, dropped the carafe at that. Monica, Vanessa and Kurt started laughing, naturally, and there was a sharp tug on the tail of my jacket from Cassie's vicinity. As for Lisa Hartwell ... well, she wasn't amused.

"We've been told you consort with the devil, Ms. Kerry," she said sharply. "We got a tip. We didn't really believe it, but now we're not so sure. How do you respond to that?"

Kurt couldn't resist. "She's got you, boss. Sleeping with women, consorting with devils, kissing TV reporters —"

"She *didn't* kiss her," Cassie snapped.

"But you don't deny the rest," he said happily. "Are you getting all this okay, Ms. Hartwell?"

To her credit, she ignored him. She was light on IQ, but at least she knew a camera hog when she saw it. *"Do* you consort with devils, Ms. Kerry?"

Monica badly wanted my attention, but I checked with Vanessa instead. Just perceptibly, she nodded. All right, then.

"Guess the jig is up," I said to the reporter. "Yes, I do. Several devils, in fact."

For a second, there was utter silence in the office except for the whir of the camera.

"Don't listen to her," Jack demanded. "She's insane. Took a bad hit on the head in a car last —"

"He's one of them," I said. "So is Jenner. And don't even get me started on Kurt here. I think he's Jack's familiar, but it's hard to —"

Cassie grabbed me, with purpose, and got between me and the camera. *"Really* don't listen to her. She gets like this sometimes. Where do you get off listening to Howard Abner anyway?"

"I can't reveal my sources," the reporter said primly. "But how do you explain what we saw when we walked in just now?"

Cassie tightened her grip, by way of warning. "Devvy's a writer. She was testing a concept. I tried to tell her we didn't *need* to set the carpet on fire, but she gets really stubborn sometimes." She punctuated "stubborn" with a fierce blue glare at me. "So you just tell Howard Abner to jam his devils and ..."

"I doubt they'd fit," I said thoughtfully.

"... get out of this office. Got that?"

The reporter shook her head. "I'm afraid I can't leave yet. Not till I get something I can use."

You could've sailed the *QEII* through the opening that comment left for Kurt. He sailed through, of course, leaving awkward silence in his wake.

"Like I said," I remarked to the reporter, "we're not really sure what he is."

He snorted. "Well, we sure as hell know what *you* are, boss."

"Kurt," Cassie warned, "I'll beat you to death with my cell phone if you say one more word."

As threats went, that wasn't much. She had the very latest, very smallest model there was; it looked like something you used to tell Scotty to beam you up. I'd told her she had reverse size envy, she'd told me I was just jealous because mine was bigger, and it had degenerated into a really stupid argument even for us.

Kurt wasn't buying it anyway. He was having too much fun. "I could say the same word about you, Cass."

The demons had been suspiciously quiet for a while. I glanced over; they were listening intently, but more like spectators than the causes of all this. A fine time for them to act normal.

"Somebody hand me my briefcase," Cassie growled. "The phone's in the key compartment."

The reporter was losing patience. "Look, I'm on deadline. Can somebody just tell me —"

"I *did* tell you," I said. "I *do* consort with devils. With demons, too. Did I leave that part out before?"

I felt the fight go out of Cassie. She sank back down on my shoulder, resigned.

"Demons?" the reporter asked.

"Demons," I confirmed, putting an arm around Cassie. "They're a little different. They're real. You see those two women?"

Everyone looked at Vanessa and Monica, who took pains to look fabulously bored.

"They're both demons. The sulky blonde is Cassie's, and the sulky brunette is mine. They have a bet about our souls. I've slept with the brunette, by the way."

That got me a dangerous whack from Cassie, but it didn't matter. The looks on everyone else's faces were worth it.

"Monica is pretty much my fault. I repressed my sex drive for six years, so she decided to get out and make me pay for it. Hell hath no fury, and all that. I happen to like the hell she raised, so I'm not complaining. Questions so far?"

Apparently not.

"Vanessa's another story. We're not sure where she came from. Cassie isn't exactly into sexual repression, so ..."

Kurt started laughing again.

"Bite me, Kurt," Cassie snapped.

"... we just work with her as best we can. So far, it's worked out fine. Cassie's demon checkmates mine, nobody goes to hell and it's more fun than therapy. Questions now?"

Lisa Hartwell looked to Cassie for help but found none. "They're really demons?"

"Yes," I said.

"Can they do something on camera to prove it?"

"I can't imagine why not. They know lots of parlor tricks."

Monica gave me a resentful look. But she pointed at Kurt, and suddenly there was a possum on the carpet, trying to dig its way out of Kurt's clothes.

So *that* was what possums were. Not a bad look for Kurt, though; those beady eyes were all him. I watched in fascination, Cassie hanging on to me for dear life, laughing so hard that she probably couldn't have stood on her own, while the thing scrabbled out of Kurt's shirt. A few feet away, the reporter was making little strangling sounds; I figured she'd be climbing up on the desk as soon as her motor skills kicked back in.

"You could have made it uglier," Vanessa said to Monica, aggrieved. "He tried to feel me up in the elevator the other day."

Monica shrugged. "I promised Devlin possums. Besides, you've kissed worse."

Vanessa huffed and puffed, but didn't actually defend herself. At the same time, Kurt started waddling toward Jack, who was frozen in horror where he stood.

"You don't think ...?" Cassie asked.

I shook my head. "The other one was supposed to be Walt. But this works, too."

Kurt sniffed Jack's expensive wingtips, tail twitching madly. Then he lunged up inside Jack's pants leg, thawing the man out in a flash. There was a brief terrible scene, Jack shrieking and trying to shake Kurt out of his pants leg, Kurt stubbornly holding on, before Jack tripped, hit a wall head-first and went down cold. Kurt promptly scampered the rest of the way up his pants.

Cassie half-collapsed in delighted hysterics, gripping my shirt. Hartwell, perhaps in shock, held her ground, and the cameraman kept shooting it all like a trouper.

"That is so *cheap,*" Vanessa grumbled.

Monica gave her a superior smile.

"Any more questions?" I asked the reporter.

She blinked a couple of times. "These are all special effects, right?"

"Oh, yes," Cassie said. "We're really good at those around here. Want to see one more?"

I didn't know about anyone else, but I'd seen more than enough for one morning. "What are you up to, Cass?"

"It's like you said, honey. We might as well be hanged for wolves." She brushed some stray hair back out of my eyes. "That's better. I want this to look good on TV. Ms. Hartwell?"

The reporter whispered to the cameraman again, and they both moved closer. "I don't believe we have your name," she said. "Would you mind —"

"Cassandra Wolfe. With an 'e.' Devvy sleeps with *me* now — not with the witch. Is that camera on?"

"Of course it is. Can I ask —"

"No," I said, finally catching Cassie's drift. "We're not taking any more questions. We're making a statement. You want ratings, correct? This is sweeps month?"

The woman tried to look offended. "We're in the news division. We report stories. The ratings —"

"Pay your salary, just like they pay ours. We're going to do you a professional courtesy, Ms. Hartwell. Do you remember the last time we met?"

That spooked her. But she did her best to look both brave and perfectly straight.

"Of course you do. Females who can't even remember who fathered their children remember this sort of thing. Not that I'm accusing you of anything. It's just a general comment."

"Get on with it," Cassie said, tugging me closer.

"It's not even just you, Ms. Hartwell. It's everyone. Two actresses kiss on prime-time TV as a ratings stunt, and the country comes to a screeching halt. You'd think nobody had ever thought of it before in real life. The hell of it was, that wasn't even a kiss. *This* is a kiss."

Cassie met me more than halfway, in the spirit of demonstration. Regrettably, the demonstration got out of hand, so we didn't quite hear the crash until a while later.

Lisa Hartwell turned out to have been what crashed; she was passed out cold on the floor. That was about right. It pretty much completed the picture: scorched carpet, bodies on the ground and something furry scavenging in Jack's trousers. I was impressed by the cameraman's control; he was still rolling. My guess was that he'd done military service — or jail time.

"This'll get on the 6:00 news?" I asked.

He didn't answer for a second, busy panning over the room. "Yep."

"And you'll make sure she gets back to the station in one piece?"

"Yep."

A man of many word. Oh, well, we were done here.

"I move that we adjourn," I said. "Let's go see Jenner. I think it's time to show him the diversity ad. One of the demons here want to do something about Kurt?"

"What for?" Cassie asked.

"I'm not carrying that thing upstairs. Look where it's been."

"Humans," Monica grumbled. But she fixed a hard red stare on Jack, and the possum crawled back out of his pants. Then she pointed at the creature, and it turned back into Kurt. Only trouble was, his clothes were in a pile on the other side of the room.

It took a few seconds for him to figure out his predicament. Maybe he was still fuzzy from being a possum. But finally, he did — and then yelped, snatched up his clothes and hightailed it out of the office.

Out in the hall, we heard female screams, followed by howling laughter.

"This has been a really interesting day so far," I said to Cassie. "Ready for Jenner?"

"This is the Monty-Fucking-Python part, right?"

"Right."

She smiled and took my arm. "Ready."

Chapter Nineteen

Like the Wizard, Jenner was in no mood to see us, but Sanchez owed me a favor. "He's got quiet time penciled in," she said, "but guess what? Pencil erases. Go right on in."

"Hold his calls?" I asked.

She sighed. "How long have I known you, Dev? I put all the lines on hold the minute you walked in."

It probably was a compliment. So I went on in, Cassie right behind me, the demons right behind her. Monica made sure that she got in ahead of Vanessa, which caused some hissing between them, but Cassie told them in no uncertain terms to save it.

Cripes, she was getting feisty. I made a note not to cross her on purpose any time soon. But as long as she was in a talking-back mood, I could try to make use of it. "Mr. Jenner?"

No sign of the man and no reply.

"Under the desk?" I suggested.

"Of all people," Vanessa said, impatient, "I would have thought *you* would have known where to look." She pointed a talon at the coat closet, and the door swung open. "Come out, Nat. There are people here to see you."

"Are they on fire?" he asked.

"Not yet. Now get out here."

He obeyed her, as though he were used to it — not a concept that I wanted to dwell on. Uncertain, he looked around the room, searching for clues as to what he was in for. "Did I call a meeting?"

"Years ago," I said, reveling in the B-movieness of it all. "Have a seat, Mr. Jenner. We'd like to show you some video."

"Where's Harper? Shouldn't he be here?"

"I imagine he'll be along any time now. Kurt, too. There was a little situation downstairs, but I'm sure this is the first place they'll come when they get everything straight."

"So to speak," Cassie added. "Sit down, Mr. Jenner."

Jenner checked with Vanessa again. She was leaning against the wall, looking implacable; when his eyes wandered down her torso, she practically slammed her jacket shut. He tried Monica next and got a flash of fangs for his trouble.

So he sat.

Good boss. Resisting the urge to pat him on the head, I stuck a tape in the VCR and waited for the monitor to warm up. "Let me bring you up to speed, Mr. Jenner. You weren't supposed to see this until Friday, but things happen. So —"

"What things?"

"Take your pick," I said. "We've got things from wall to wall. Baptists and devils and lunatic clients and girl reporters in closets and your creative director passed out downstairs with my copywriter up his shorts. Where do you want to start?"

His brow furrowed painfully. Too many words. "Miss Wolfe? Do you understand Derry?"

"Yes. But I love her anyway."

I gave her a bad look for that. She just laughed, though, and nodded at the monitor. Conditioned as I was, I half-expected it to start playing all by itself. But it would be best if she never, ever, *ever* found that out. So I got the remote off Jenner's desk and started the VCR the hard way.

∞ ∞ ∞

It was child's play, after all. Jenner folded like a cheap tent a few seconds into the tape, and he was still in a fetal position several minutes later, when Jack and Kurt finally got there.

"Hello again, Jack," Cassie said. "You look terrible."

He *did* look terrible. For one thing, his fly was still open, but that was such a small detail. It was all he could do to make it to Jenner's desk. "Call the police, Mr. Jenner."

Jenner didn't hear that. He was curled up tight in his chair, rocking gently, trying to forget.

"Call the police," Jack repeated. "They're witches."

"Demons," Monica growled.

Kurt caught sight of her and yelped. But before he could run, Vanessa pointed at the door, which promptly closed with a bang. For good measure, the deadbolt turned, too.

"Mr. Jenner?" Jack slapped his face, tentatively at first, then harder. "Nat? Are you in there? We've got to call the police."

"The police can't help him," I said. "They can't help you two, either."

Cassie nodded. "Way too late for that."

"Even if they could, they wouldn't believe you." Comfortably, I settled an arm around Cassie, who'd been leaning against my shoulder. "Grown men, seeing demons. Not to mention the part about the possum."

Over in the far corner, Kurt sank to the carpet, clearly in distress. Jack shook Jenner with purpose.

"It looked lovesick to me," Cassie said to me. "Didn't you think so, honey?"

"It was certainly in a hurry."

"Snap out of it," Jack urged Jenner. "The police won't come unless *you* call. Not after the last time."

Cassie was as happy as I'd seen her in days. "He's not listening to us, Devvy. Should we turn them over to the witches?"

"Keep it up, girlie," Monica warned.

"The demons, you mean, sweetheart. We could do that if you want. Or turn the demons over to them. I don't think it matters now."

"Kurt, goddamn you, call 911!" Jack shouted, still shaking Jenner. "Tell them you're him!"

Kurt didn't answer. He was crouched down in the corner as though it might be safe there.

"Let's give them to Monica," Cassie suggested. "Maybe they'll give her heartburn."

"Or we could keep them as pets."

"Not at *my* house."

I let it go at that. I'd have a talk with Vanessa later about the logistics of it, though. Maybe she could shrink them down to a size I could keep in a terrarium on my desk. The idea of feeding flies to Kurt with tweezers was weirdly appealing. Not too many flies, though; he could stand to drop a few pounds.

Jack, sweating heavily now, gave Jenner one last slap and then threw his limp body back into his chair. "Dammit, Kerry, what did you do to him?"

"The same thing I'm about to do to you," I said. "Have a chair. Let's see some video."

"What video?"

"The diversity ad, Jack. Surely you remember. Our public-service announcement on what is and is not normal. You might want to take notes."

Scowling, he wiped his damp forehead. "Normal? What would *you* know about it?"

Good thing I already had a grip on Cassie; she almost got loose, and it wouldn't have been pretty. "There's no such thing as normal, Jack. There's only an average of deviance. And around this place, I figure that Cassie and I are it."

"What the hell does *that* mean?"

"Just watch the tape."

Vanessa made a great production of clearing her throat.

"On second thought," I said, watching her carefully, "let's watch it on live TV."

Cassie, who hadn't known about that part, started laughing.

"Who's got the remote?"

"Amateur," Vanessa said, pointing. The TV flashed on and started changing channels. Some cooking show, a cartoon, "I Love Lucy," people throwing chairs around on some talk show ...

... and Kathie Lee Gifford.

"No," Cassie said, sounding very definite.

I checked my watch. "Just a few seconds of it. Jack? Can you see all right? How about you, Kurt?"

Neither of them answered. Jack was slumped against the wall, a picture of defeat with hair plugs, and Kurt was still balled up in the far corner of the office, but they were both focused on the TV screen. As the show broke for commercials, their vital signs picked up visibly. You can always tell advertising professionals.

As for Monica, the light had just begun to dawn on her, and by the way she was looking at Vanessa, we were in for a storm. "You can't do this," she said to her.

"Of course I can."

"You can't *do* it," Monica insisted. *"Devlin's* on that tape, too. She can't out herself on purpose. That would make me —"

"Unnecessary," Cassie said. "Yes. We know."

Monica glared at her, then back at Vanessa. "You can't do it. You're a demon. You can't help her. It's not *done.*"

" 'Can't' be damned. I never liked you, Monica."

"Break my heart. *I* never liked *you.*"

"Quiet," I said to them, watching the TV. "It's on."

So we all watched. It was nothing outré, really — just a day in the life of J/J/G, complete with bone-sucking, cross-dressing, adultery in a supply room, adultery in a conference room, adultery in a men's room ... and a little digitally assisted magic between Jenner and Howard Abner, all of it cut to "I Enjoy Being a Girl." Connie the Barbarian had given me the idea, after all. Critically, I studied the segment in which Jack was dancing with Kester the mortician, wondering whether chiffon had been the wrong fabric for Kester or whether the problem was just the color.

"You can't *do* this," Monica repeated.

But she — we — already had. The next clip was that kiss from the security-camera tape.

"You might want to re-cut it later, Devvy," Cassie said. "Channel 12 just got some *much* better film of us."

Suddenly, Monica shrieked, very much like the Wicked Witch of the West. We heard a pop, followed by a wet sound, and she was gone.

"Never liked her much," Vanessa said casually, wiping her hands.

Instinctively, I turned toward the corner. Kurt looked as though something had gone down the wrong way. His eyes seemed a bit bloodshot, too. But he was still staring at the TV screen, which was showing the final title: "What do you enjoy being?"

Jack, of course, had fainted again.

Vanessa crossed over to him, nudged him with the pointy toe of her shoe and smiled in satisfaction. "Well, that was fun. Now, who wants to go out for mochaccino?"

"Not so fast," I said. "We've got to explain all this somehow."

"No, you don't. Besides, where would you start?"

Cassie and I looked at each other for a long time, thinking it over. Where *would* we start? And what, after all, would be the point?

"She's a demon," Cassie finally said. "We'll let her handle it."

So we let her, and she did.

∞ ∞ ∞

An hour later, we were standing in the parking lot waiting for Vanessa. She was just tidying up a few last details in the office, she said, and it wouldn't take a minute.

Finally, we heard a screech of tires and turned to find Vanessa barreling down on us at the wheel of a bright-red BMW convertible. I gave her the benefit of the doubt for two seconds, then grabbed Cassie and pulled us both to safety.

"Whoops," Vanessa said while the car rocked to a stop. "Haven't driven one of these in a while. Everyone all right?"

"No thanks to you," I grumbled.

"Oh, stop griping. I fixed everything, didn't I? Anyway, you're on vacation now. Here."

Cassie reached around me and took the tickets, checking the times against her watch. "This is cutting it close, Vanessa. We're barely going to have time to —"

"You're already packed. I handled it. The bags are in your trunk."

"For both of us? For Kansas City, too?"

"I *said*, I handled it. Now, get going. You'll miss your plane."

"Not if *I* drive," Cassie observed.

Vanessa gunned the motor. "Buckle up, then, Devlin. See you at the beach."

I squinted into the sun after her. It might have been my imagination, but I would've sworn that there was a Jesus fish on the back of Vanessa's car.

Chapter Twenty

Saturday
On the Beach

Cassie stretched luxuriously and reached over to the little table for her margarita. Suspicious, I lifted the brim of my hat a couple of inches to count the leftover slices of lime. Was that three for her now, or four?

"Prohibition's over," she said. "I thought you'd heard."

"I didn't say anything."

She made a moué and offered me the glass. Well, it was the least I could do. Couldn't have her getting tequila poisoning. "Cheers," I said.

"Thanks. Don't mind if I do." Then she reached down to the sand beside her and brought up another margarita.

I regarded her in silence. I'd taken a nap for — what, fifteen minutes? — and she'd already opened her own beachfront saloon. Cassandra's-by-the-Sea. Margaritas from coast to coast, no waiting, no cover ...

Definitely no cover. Frowning slightly, I pulled my hat brim back down. At least I'd had the sense to put on the hat and a T-shirt after that last swim. It was a very bright day, and there was way too much of her showing in that swimsuit. Especially when she stretched like that, and especially because she kept *doing* it. The college boys on the blanket down the way had practically sprained their eyeballs gawking. Right now, they were playing some loud stupid game with a Frisbee, trying to get her attention.

Blissfully oblivious, Cassie lowered her glass. She licked her lips. "This margarita is defective. I think I should have it replaced. What do *you* think?"

"I think you should put on your T-shirt," I said seriously.

"Later. But only if you promise to take it off."

"Cassie ..."

"With no hands."

Guiltily, I checked to see whether anyone might have heard that. She just smirked, though, and leaned over the arm of her chair to kiss me. She took her time about it, too. Well, all right, fine — probably nobody could see much, what with the umbrella behind us. And it wasn't like we'd never done this in public before. Sometimes I wondered whether we should start charging admission.

"You're causing a scene," a familiar voice said. "That boy in the orange trunks just hit a dog with a Frisbee."

We both jumped a little. Vanessa had set up shop in a beach chair next to us, complete with a tiny swimsuit and a large umbrella.

"Are you going to tag along this whole vacation?" I asked, annoyed.

"Of course not. You couldn't get me to go to Kansas City for all the souls in the world."

Cassie bristled a little. "It's a nice town, Vanessa."

"I'm not talking about the town. I'm talking about Thanksgiving dinner with your family. You and pookie are on your own for that."

"Don't call me pookie," I snapped.

"Lighten up, would you? This is a vacation. Speaking of which ..." She raised her hand; a cute pink drink appeared in it. "That's more like it. Anyone else?"

"I could use another margarita, thanks," Cassie said. "And pookie here —"

Another, even more familiar voice broke in. "So. *There* you are."

Uh-oh.

My personal demon slogged the last few steps toward us through the sand, shoes in one hand, hem of her long black gown in the other, looking extremely put out.

Cassie rounded on Vanessa. "I thought you got *rid* of her. I *thought* you said —"

The demon shrugged. "Temporary. Don't worry. I can always do it again."

"You are all in serious trouble with me," Monica said ominously. "Especially *you,* you cheap little soul-stealing slut."

"Lovely to see you, too, sweetie darling," Vanessa replied. "Little drinkie?"

Monica ignored that. She swatted as much sand off her gown as she could, glaring first at Cassie and me, then at Vanessa, then back at us.

"For God's sake, sit down," I finally said. "You're blocking Cassie's sun. What can we get you? Margarita? Daiquiri? Human blood?"

She ignored that, too. "That was a very cheap trick, Vanessa. Driving me into that Kurt person. Slippery little bastard — I had Satan's own time getting out. On *top* of which, we wound up in bed with Jack Harper first."

Cassie started laughing like she would never stop. I couldn't help but smile a little myself.

"I'm not forgetting this," Monica warned.

"I don't see how you could," Vanessa agreed, stirring her drink with the paper parasol. "Now go away. I'm on vacation."

Monica's eyes glowed red, and she raised a hand in a menacing way, which was enough for me to leap over the chair arm to get Cassie covered up. But Vanessa just whistled, and a passing seagull wheeled around.

"You wouldn't dare," Monica said to her.

"Wrong," she said, pointing with the end of the little parasol.

There was that pop again. The gull squawked in outrage and flew in a few angry circles. Then it started chasing a fat man in a beer-can hat down the beach.

Cassie gently pushed me off, the better to see. "She's really in that seagull?"

"She'll get back out again," Vanessa said, "but let her eat garbage for a while. What's the matter, Devlin? You look troubled."

"I don't think I like Monica popping in and out of things. It makes life too unpredictable."

"Life *is* unpredictable. Yours more than most people's, of course. But then, you're not most people."

No, I wasn't, at that. Most people would have jumped off a bridge by now, preferring the certainty of death to the past few months of my life. On the other hand ...

I glanced at Cassie. She tilted her head a little and gave me one of those smiles that made my heart do funny things. On the other hand, I wouldn't have missed this for the world.

"To hell with most people," I said, "and damn everything but Cass."

Cassie laughed. "I love you, too."

"This could be the start of a beautiful relationship," Vanessa declared, raising her glass. "For all of us. Well, all of us except the witch. Cheers!"

About the Author

Photo by Ian Rowan
The bears in question are named —
by the manufacturer —
Devlin and Cassandra

The Average of Deviance is the direct result of *Several Devils*, which was the result of K. Simpson's seeing *Bram Stoker's Dracula* one too many times in the fall of 1992. The whole Devil's Workshop series essentially started there.

Or maybe it started in childhood. Simpson always loved Halloween, ghost stories and vampire movies; she still likes almost everything in that genre, from Edgar Allan Poe to Elvira. She thinks it's all a form of theater, which may be why it appeals to her.

She has no known personal demons, doesn't worship the Devil and doesn't work for an ad agency. But she is from the Midwest and does know a little too much about advertising people. She's even worked for companies so crazy that they make J/J/G look like IBM.

That's not necessarily a bad thing. She hates being bored.

Also by K. Simpson

Several Devils
Published: August 2001
ISBN: 0967768799

Even though she's in advertising, Devlin Kerry doesn't believe in Hell; she thinks that would be redundant. But a demon named Monica believes in her. Between her demon and her best friend, Dev's in for a devil of a time.

Now Available from Fortitude Press

THE BLUEST EYES IN TEXAS
BY LINDA CRIST

Kennedy Nocona is an out, liberal, driven attorney, living in Austin, the heart of the Texas hill country. Once a player in the legal community, she now finds herself in the position of re-evaluating her life - a position brought on by a personal tragedy for which she blames herself. Seeking redemption for her tormented past, she loses herself in her work, strict discipline of mind and body, and the teachings of Native American roots she once shunned.

Dallasite Carson Garret is a young paralegal overcoming the loss of her parents and coming to terms with her own sexual orientation. After settling her parents' estate and examining her failed past relationships, she is desperately ready to move forward. Bored with her state of affairs, she longs for excitement and romance to make her feel alive again.

A chance encounter finds them inexplicably drawn to one another, and after a weekend together, they quickly find themselves in a long distance romance that leaves them both wanting more. Circumstances at Carson's job develop into a series of mysteries and blackmail attempts that leaves her with more excitement than she ever bargained for. Confused, afraid, and alone, she turns to Kennedy, the one person she knows can help her. As they work together to solve a puzzle, they confront growing feelings that neither woman can deny, complicated by outside forces that threaten to crush them both.

ISBN: 0971815003

Now Available from Fortitude Press

I Found My Heart In San Francisco
by S.X. Meagher

Despite the questions of her roommates and the objections of her fiancé, Jamie Evans persists in enrolling in a college course that seems an odd choice for a young woman of her background. What no one can know is that the course, The Psychology of the Lesbian Experience, will propel Jamie onto a journey of self-awareness and realization.

For the required fieldwork, Jamie is paired with the darkly beautiful Ryan O'Flaherty —a boldly "out" and sexually adventurous lesbian. This somewhat unlikely pair slowly, and sometimes painfully become aware that what they feel for each other is more than just friendship.

The temptation to live life on her own terms is great, but so are the costs, as Jamie struggles to break out of her establishment-fashioned, pre-ordained mold. If she can summon the courage, however, she might find out that love, and life, have so much more to offer than she had ever dreamed.

ISBN: 0971815038

Now Available from Fortitude Press

WARLORD METAL
BY D. JORDAN REDHAWK

The heavy metal band, Warlord, is in need of a new guitarist. Only one applicant stands out – a jewel in the very rough – Torrin Smith. She has the ability to make her guitar sing her soul – a sinister and shattered cry.

Sonny Middlestead, little sister to a member of the band, is making her way through high school in accelerated learning classes. Her days are filled with education, her nights with rock and roll. An aspiring journalist, she spends a good deal of her free time writing in her diary.

The two meet – dark and light, anger and love – with both disastrous and remarkable potential. Will Torrin be swept away by her substance abuse, unable to release her fury or accept the brightness of another's heart? Can Sonny find a way to heal a broken childhood, to make up for a lifetime of injustice and hate?

Only time will tell.

ISBN: 097181502X

Also by D. Jordan Redhawk

TIOPA KI LAKOTA
Published: October 2000
ISBN: 1930928033

Anpo, a Lakota woman raised as a warrior, rescues Kathleen, the golden-haired woman of her vision. A vision that includes not only Kathleen's coming, but also the infliction of great pain. Must all dreams come true?

Now Distributed by Fortitude Press

AT FIRST BLUSH
A JANE DOE PRESS ANTHOLOGY

Twenty-two stories of first glances, first blushes, first loves and first times - of all kinds. Representing a variety of voices, the stories reflect a diversity of experiences. All profits from this anthology will be donated to charity.

The table of contents from this wonderful collection of stories:

ISBN: 0971154996

Now Distributed by Fortitude Press

CONSPIRACY OF SWORDS
BY R.S. CORLISS

FBI Agent Alexia Reis is an out-lesbian determined to make it in the bureau. As a junior agent she spent time in the research department, as well as the serial crimes unit where she and her partner, David Wu, were recognized for their work. After breaking several major cases, the two are moved to the hate crimes unit, which is Alex's true area of expertise.

Following the murders of several prominent activists and politicians, Alex and David become part of a task force charged with solving the killings. Together, they are sent to protect a newly declared candidate for the U.S. Senate. For the first time in her career, Alex is named the agent-in-charge, and when the candidate is assassinated, she can't help but take it personally.

During the investigation the agents run into ex-CIA assassin Teren Mylos, who is convinced her partner's death is somehow connected to the FBI case. While wary of each other, Alex and Teren agree to share information in an attempt to find answers to the deepening mystery.

The case takes them to Europe and back, searching for pieces to the unfolding puzzle. As they dodge killers and turncoats, they come face to face with Nazis old and new, stumble upon a hoard of looted gold, and uncover a conspiracy that stretches over forty years and two continents.

And, somewhere along the line, they discover each other as well.

ISBN: 0971154902

Now Distributed by Fortitude Press

EXCHANGES
BY JOHN-DAVID SCHRAMM

Can God change gays? This question tumbles around inside the minds of both lead characters in *exChanges*.

Marcus and CJ both give up a great deal to join Crossroads, a year-long, residential program dedicated to helping gay men and lesbians find "freedom" from homosexuality through the power of Christ.

"Camping out" with five other men and a house leader, CJ and Marcus begin to confront themselves while being strangely drawn to one another.

Follow these two men as they dive into the rules and policies of this ministry program led by former drag queens and pornography kings. As each man confronts his own issues, he begins to see a path that could never have been covered in the Crossroads recruiting brochure.

ISBN: 0971154937

To Order:

Title	Quantity	Cost per Unit	Total Cost
The Average of Deviance		$12.99	$
At First Blush		$21.99	$
The Bluest Eyes in Texas		$15.99	$
Conspiracy of Swords		$19.99	$
exChanges		$13.75	$
I Found My Heart in San Francisco		$18.99	$
The Life in Her Eyes		$13.99	$
Warlord Metal		$13,99	$
Shipping and Handling	First Book	$4.50	$
	Each Add'l Book	$2.00	$
	Texas Residents Add 8.25% Sales Tax		$
		Total	$

To order by credit card, please visit our Web site at:
www.fortitudepress.com.

To order by check or money order, please mail the above form to:

Fortitude Press, Inc.
Post Office Box 41
Melbourne, FL 32902

Coming Soon from Fortitude Press

ENGRAVINGS OF WRAITH
BY KIERA DELLACROIX

Bailey Cameron is a woman with secrets. The reclusive owner of a successful corporation, she is also hostage to a covert life she neither wanted nor asked for, one that refuses to become a part of her past.

Blackmailed into a return to her deadly role as The Wraith, a frightening entity in the world that lives in the shadows, Bailey decides to break free. She settles in for a brutal game of chess with her former employers, prepared for every eventuality but one -- Piper Tate, her new assistant who decides that the dark, mysterious Bailey is someone she wants to know better. A lot better.

The stakes continue to rise, as Piper peels away the layers that have protected Bailey. She discovers a gentle, innocent heart -- beating within the body of a killer who can't be tamed and who is prepared to do whatever it takes to preserve the new world Piper has introduced her to.

Coming Soon from Fortitude Press

MIND GAMES
BY RYAN DALY

Rachel "Tuck" Tucker is a high-powered player in the world of investment banking. Ruthless and beautiful, she goes through bank accounts and women at lightning speed. Yet her wealth comes from insider trading, in the most literal of senses.

Since childhood, Tuck has been gifted with the ability to leave her physical body and take over other people's, imposing her considerable and decidedly devious will on their actions while leaving them none the wiser. She has used her ability for wealth and pleasure, never giving any thought to those she used along the way.

Her world changes rapidly when she becomes trapped in a body not her own. Complicating things further, she's stuck inside a man. A married man. With children.

Working against time and forces she doesn't understand, Tuck struggles to return to herself. But doing so would almost certainly mean losing her accidental life and Kate, the wife of the man she's replaced. A choice that becomes harder for Tuck with each day spent with her new family.

An intriguing novel of suspense and romance, *Mind Games* shows why it's always better to be yourself.